Charlie,
Keep on thinkin'
about Abraham Lincoln!
Betty Kay
2007

What Did Lincoln Do...
In 1832?
In 1842?
In 1862?

By

Betty Carlson Kay

1663 LIBERTY DRIVE, SUITE 200
BLOOMINGTON, INDIANA 47403
(800) 839-8640
WWW.AUTHORHOUSE.COM

© 2004 Betty Carlson Kay
All Rights Reserved.

No part of this book may be reproduced, stored in a retrieval system, or transmitted by any means without the written permission of the author.

First published by AuthorHouse 11/15/04

ISBN: 1-4208-0286-0 (sc)

Library of Congress Control Number: 2004097839

Printed in the United States of America
Bloomington, Indiana

This book is printed on acid-free paper.

Other books by Betty Carlson Kay

Americans of Character Series
Abraham Lincoln

Harriet Tubman

Roberto Clemente

Maya Lin

Chief Joseph

Illinois from A to Z

Jacksonville, The Traditions Continue

Cicero, The First Suburb West

This is a work of Historical Fiction.

Cover photo: This statue of Abraham Lincoln as a 23-year-old volunteer soldier in the Black Hawk War stands in Dixon, Illinois.

Contents

I. What Did Lincoln Do In 1832?

January:	Meet the Rutledge Family	3
February:	Snow Storm	8
March:	Lincoln Pilots The Talisman Steamboat	15
April:	New Salem Troops Muster for Black Hawk	21
May:	Spelling Bee	25
June:	At the Mill	30
July:	Lincoln Returns to New Salem	35
August:	Church "Camp Meeting"	40
September:	Lincoln at his Berry-Lincoln General Store	45
October:	Lincoln Takes Up Surveying	50
November:	Lincoln Takes Election Returns to Springfield	55
December:	Lincoln Studies Law	60
The Rutledge Family Tree		65
Notes:		66

II. What Did Lincoln Do in 1842?

January:	Meet Jed, the Journal Writer	69
February:	Lincoln at Washington Temperance Society	71
March:	Lincoln Partners with Stephen T. Logan	74
April:	The Spring Circuit	77
May:	Spring Fever	79
June:	Lincoln Speaks of his "National Debt"	81
July:	Jed Goes Hunting	84
August:	"Rebecca" Letters	86
September:	The Lincoln-Shields Duel	89
October:	The Fall Circuit	92
November:	Abraham Lincoln Marries Mary Todd	95
December:	Jed's Growing Pains	98
Notes:		102

III. What Did Lincoln Do in 1862?

January:	Meet Tad Lincoln	107
February:	Willie Dies	111
March:	Life Without Willie	113
April:	The Merrimack Attacks Union Ships	115
May:	Lincoln Has Adventures Running the War	118
June:	Mrs. Lincoln Visits Spiritualists	120
July:	The Lincoln Family at The Soldier's Home	123
August:	Meet Colonel Thaddeus Lowe	125
September:	Meet Colonel Benjamin Grierson	128
October:	Writing the Emancipation Proclamation	130
November:	Tad Goes with Mrs. Lincoln to NYC	132
December:	Lincoln and the Sioux Indian Uprising	134
The Story Ends		137
Notes:		139

What Did Lincoln Do In 1832?

Betty Carlson Kay

The Rutledge Inn

January 1832

"Happy New Year!" called Mother to Nancy and Peggy. "Come on, sleepyheads, get up and push your little trundle bed under the big bed. Then pull the covers up smooth and nice. It's 1832, so let's start off the new year right!"

"Happy New Year," Mother then repeated to every guest as he came down the ladder at the Rutledge Inn. "Happy New Year to you, too, Mrs. Rutledge," said the men. Though it was still early in the morning, Mother had been up before anyone else, cooking breakfast for the family and the boarders.

Nineteen-year-old Ann Rutledge, quickly tied her clean apron over her not-so-clean dress and stepped into the kitchen to help. She put on her white day cap to keep the soot out of her hair. The young girls were a bit slower getting out of bed and rubbed their eyes and yawned.

Ten-year-old Nancy and eight-year-old Peggy peered at each other from under their white nightcaps. "Let's make a wish for the new year before we get up," said Nancy.

Peggy giggled. She was always wishing for things that couldn't possibly come true, but today she would wish for something that just might. "I wish that we could have some white sugar today!"

Nancy smiled. "Oh, that would be lovely on the first day of the new year!" she agreed.

The girls tucked in their blankets and pushed their bed under the high bed. Then they tied each other's apron bows in the back and quickly washed their faces in the bowl of chilly water. They skipped into the kitchen to see who was eating breakfast. Mother and Ann were busy cooking and serving about five boarders. Father and the older boys were out doing chores and William was getting in everyone's way. "Mind your little brother for me girls," said Mother.

Nancy and Peggy put William in his chair, and politely greeted the men. They were used to having lots of people around in their log house in New Salem. After all, there were nine children in their family! And, since their parents ran the only inn in the town, there were always extra guests upstairs in the loft.

One fella had been boarding with them a lot recently. He was tall and thin, and laughed easily. The way he played with little William, they figured he missed having his own family around quite a bit. His name was Mr. Lincoln, but he told them they could call him Abraham. He slept in Mr. Offut's store where he was clerking, but he sometimes took his meals at the Rutledge Inn.

While Nancy and Peggy ate their mush (corn meal soaked in milk), the door opened and in came their brothers, David and Robert. The cold January wind blew in with them. They carried arm loads of wood and with their red cheeks and laughing eyes, they filled the room with energy.

"The well's froze up, ma, so after breakfast we'll go down to the river to get a bucket water," said David. "It's getting right cold out there."

"Well, I guess we can stand the cold," said Mother, "as long as we don't have a big snow like last winter. It wasn't fit for man or beast."

"I reckon you're right, ma'am" said Abraham. "We was trying to get a flatboat down the Sangamon River last spring and the melting water and flooding held us up."

Ann interrupted, "You mean, we WERE trying to get the boat down the river."

"You're right, we WERE!" laughed Abraham. "I am studying on my grammar and I thank you, ma'am for your help."

"Any way you say it, it means the same thing," said Mother. "That was a real bad winter. But this year seems different. No snow at all yet. Maybe we'll get lucky and have a nice easy winter for a change."

"Can Nancy and I go down to the river with the boys, please, Ma?" asked Peggy.

"If you do your chores first and bundle up real good, I don't see why not. Go ahead," answered Mother.

The girls hurried with their chores while their brothers, David and Robert, ate breakfast. Nancy and Peggy cleared the table and swept the floor. They helped William and Sallie finish their breakfasts, and then they hurried to bundle up.

Each girl put on a second pair of stockings, a second flannel petticoat, a second dress, their coats, bonnets, scarves and mittens. Wearing so many clothes made it hard to bend over but the sisters laughed and skipped out the door with their brothers.

"Race you to the river," teased Robert. "Last one there has to carry the bucket home!"

"No fair!" cried the girls, but they ran as fast as they could anyway.

The river was not far but it was down a big hill. They ran faster and faster, no one wanting to be the last one there. The older boys won easily, and as the girls caught up to them, the brothers handed them the bucket. Robert had the axe to chop the frozen edge of the ice, and soon there was a hole big enough for the bucket. But as Peggy leaned over, her foot slipped on the icy rocks and before she knew it, she was up to her knees in freezing cold water!

David grabbed the bucket from her, Robert grabbed one hand, and Nancy grabbed her other hand. They had their little sister out in no time, but the damage was done. She was soaked to the skin and still had to walk back up the hill to their house.

There was nothing to do but run, pulling Peggy as fast as they could. As she got colder and colder, her feet didn't want to move very fast and although she tried not to, she started to cry. David set the bucket down and joined in the tug-of-war to keep her legs moving and get her home. They knew that once they got her home, Mother would know what to do.

And Mother did know what to do. Off came the wet clothes, on came a warm blanket, and soon Peggy was sitting in front of the fire with a cup of hot camomile tea in her hands. Mother smiled and shook her head at the tired, sad little girl, and then she reached up for the tin that held the precious white sugar.

"This should help the medicine go down," she said as she put a teaspoonful in the cup.

Nancy laughed too. "That's getting your New Year's wish the hard way!" she said.

Dr. Allen's House

February 1832

"There's no school today!" called David and Robert as they blew into the two-room log house with the wind and the snow. Their morning chores were done, and now that the horses and cows were fed, the boys were ready to be fed too.

"How do you know?" asked Peggy. No one loved school more than Peggy did, and she hated to miss even one day. As she peeked out the window, she could see that the snow was piled up high.

"We saw Dr. Allen coming home from Carter's farm. He said the Carter's had a whale of a baby boy last night, right in the middle of the snow storm. Dr. Allen looked beat and so did his horse, what with carrying both him and a big sack of corn meal all the way into town. Paying him in money would have been a whole lot easier to tote around, but I guess getting paid in cornmeal is better than not getting paid at all!" said David.

"He's the one who told us there was no school today. Even old Mentor Graham didn't want to go out in this weather," added Robert.

"Oh, dear," sighed Peggy. It looked like it would be a long day. She knew she'd have to spend a good bit of it working on her stitching sampler. Getting her stitches nice and neat was hard for her little fingers. The fabric always seemed to end up with puckers where it should have been smooth.

Mother looked at her daughters and smiled. Today there would be no boarders coming to The Rutledge Inn. Not in such a storm. Even Mr. Lincoln would probably stay indoors, studying on his grammar or surveying books. Dinner would be just the family. All of the children could sit down and eat together without eating in shifts. Mother looked forward to a quiet day.

When she looked in the tall wooden cupboard, she spied two green glass jars of grapes she had put up last summer.

"We'll have grapes today, girls, and we'll have enough to share with the Carter's. The boys can run some food out to them this afternoon. Mrs. Carter will appreciate some extra food on her baby's birth day. Then we can celebrate too."

"What will we celebrate Mother?" asked Nancy. "It's not Christmas, and it's no one's birthday in our family, is it?"

"You'll just have to wait and see," Mother laughed.

The girls settled down to sew. Robert and David went out to chop wood. Ann was busy mending some clothes that still had some wear in them. She was gently ripping out the seams of a very faded, green calico dress. Then she turned it inside-out and outside-in and sewed the dress back together again! It looked good as new.

"That looks beautiful again," exclaimed Peggy.

"It's amazing what you can do when you want to," said Ann. "And it's amazing what you can do when the closest dress shop is 100 miles away in St. Louis."

Nancy and Peggy were sitting close to the fireplace with their sewing in their laps. The light from the fireplace and the light from the window nearby helped them see. Each girl was making a "sampler." They were stitching the letters of the alphabet, the numbers up to ten, and their own names and birth dates on a square of muslin. They used a cross stitch on the letters of the alphabet and the girls were getting pretty good at that. Their feather stitches were pretty good too. But oh, those French knots!

"I'll give you a tip," said Ann. As the oldest girl in the family now, she knew a lot about sewing. "When you make the French knot, wrap the thread around the needle three times and then <u>slowly</u> pull the needle through the fabric but not in the same hole you came up in. Go down right next to where you came up. There, now, you are doing well. Pull gently now. Watch closely as the knot begins to form. Hooray! You did it!"

Peggy and Nancy both were smiling. Maybe sewing wasn't so bad, sometimes.

"Time to cook our dinner, girls. Move away from the fireplace," said Mother.

Ann added logs to the fire and soon had it blazing. Mother sliced a thick slice of ham and cooked it in the skillet. From the cold cellar, the girls brought up potatoes and dried peas. The potatoes and peas went in a black kettle filled with boiling water hanging across the fireplace on an iron rod.

While dinner was cooking, Mother mixed cornmeal, water and salt together into a thick dough. Next, she patted a small ball of dough back and forth from hand to hand, to make it flat and round. On the last pat, she made sure she left her fingerprints on the biscuit and then she tossed it into the greased skillet sizzling in the fire. She let the little girls each make their own dodgers, with their own little fingerprints showing. Then, Mother put the lid on the skillet and shoveled coals on top of the lid to bake the bread. When a dozen dodgers were baked, Mother called them all to the table for dinner.

Father had been working down at the gristmill which he owned with Mr. Cameron. They were doing some repairs before their busy season began in the spring. When Father noticed the family dinner and the special preserved grapes on the table, he asked, "What's the special occasion?"

Mother said, "Have you not remembered that today is February 22?"

"Oh, of course!" he smiled. "It is the birthday of the first president of the United States, General George Washington."

"Aw, what's so big about that?" asked Robert.

"Well, it's a good day to remember the history of our country and the history of our Rutledge family," said Father. "Do you recall that I was born and raised back in South Carolina, and that my kin, John and Edward Rutledge, were both governors of the state of South Carolina and that Edward was a signer of the Declaration of Independence? They knew Washington well and held him in highest esteem."

"Then why don't we still live in South Carolina, Father?" asked David.

"Times change, son. The land gets all parceled up and what's left is too expensive to buy. So, we packed up and moved to Georgia, then to Tennessee, then to Kentucky, where Jane, John and Ann were born. We just kept looking for the best place to be. Then we moved on to White County, Illinois where you and Robert, Nancy and Peggy were born. Finally, we got here to New Salem where William and Sallie were born. Here we have the Inn, a nice farm at Concord, and kin nearby."

"Are we going to be moving again, Pa?" asked Nancy. Before he could answer there was a knock on the door.

"Now who could be coming to the Inn on a day like this?" he wondered. Father opened the door to find a whole family in a Conestoga wagon!

"Well, I'll be!" exclaimed Father. "What are you folks doing out in weather like this? You'd better come inside and warm up!" And that was the end of Mother's peaceful day. As innkeepers, they opened their home to travelers and locals who needed a place to stay. So, immediately, the Rutledge family sprang into action. They helped the folks in, stabled and fed their horses, and provided a friendly ear to hear their story. As soon as each guest was warming by the fire with a cup of hot coffee (half hot milk for the children), Mr. Clarke began his tale.

"We thought we were being smart, by getting an early spring start. We're heading to St. Louis, and then out west, you see. The weather's been so fine, we thought we'd have no trouble. When suddenly, this snow storm took us by surprise. We tried to sleep last night in our wagon under some trees. We did all right in the wagon, but our poor horses took a real beating. We followed some tracks today, when the storm let up, hoping that the horses wouldn't give out until we found shelter. We sure are thankful to have found you!" said Mr. Clarke.

"Give the horses a couple days' rest and they'll be good as new," said Father. "You are our only guests now, so there's plenty of room."

"Yes," said Mother. "The men can sleep up the ladder in the loft, and the women can sleep with us girls in the bedroom."

While they were talking, the Clarke baby fussed and fussed. She was more than just tired, Mother could tell.

"May I make her a spoon of medicine?" asked Mother. "Old Granny Spears has taught me many Indian cures, and they really do work." She poured hot water over crushed wild dill seeds, and gave the baby a spoonful. Soon, the baby calmed down and was sleeping soundly.

"I'll remember that trick!" said Mrs. Clarke with a grateful smile.

Nancy and Peggy were sad to see the Clarke family leave a few days later. The family and their animals all looked strong

Betty Carlson Kay

and healthy. And though they said they'd see the Rutledges again sometime, everyone knew that there was little chance of that.

The Schoolhouse

March 1832

"I am tired of mud!" said Peggy. "There's mud on my shoes, mud on my skirt and now there's mud on our slate."

"It must be March in Illinois," laughed Nancy. The two sisters were usually best friends and this was a best friends day.

They walked together to school every day, following Main Street west to the fork in the road. Since their house was at the east end of Main Street, the girls passed by almost every log house in the little town of New Salem. They knew everyone in town, and everyone knew them. Sometimes they heard a mother's voice saying, "There go the little Rutledge girls, you'd better get on the stick!" Soon, another child would come running down Main Street to catch up with them.

"I'll help you clean the slate," said Nancy, "if you'll help me with my spelling. I can remember the letters in O-R-A-N-G-E but I can't remember the order they come in!"

"Thanks," said Peggy. "Mentor Graham will give me a black mark if I come in muddy one more time."

They used leaves and grass to clean the mud off their shoes and the slate and hurried into school with the other children.

Nancy and Peggy sat down on the middle half-log bench. The littlest children sat on the smallest half-log bench in the front; the middle-sized children sat on the middle-sized bench; and the biggest children sat on the third bench, made from a very big log so that even when cut in half, it was high enough for them to easily see over the heads of the other children.

The children were buzzing today. Spring was in the air. Everyone was talking about the wrestling match the night before. The Clary's Grove boys had been in town, bragging about being so tough that no town boy dared to fight them. One of the New Salem boys had grown so much over the winter that he figured he was big enough and strong enough to whip the country boys and show them that the town boys were tough too.

The yelling and bragging went on and on until the young town boy couldn't stand it any longer. Billy took off his shirt and jumped in the ring, just as his mother came running out to see what the excitement was all about. "Keep your shirt on!" she yelled, but it was too late.

The fight didn't last long. Billy really had no chance against Jack Armstrong, the best wrestler of the bunch. There was just a little sweating, and wrestling, and grabbing, and pulling … and then, there was laughing and teasing as Jack lifted Billy up and dropped him in the horses' watering trough! As an old man helped him out, he said, "Son, don't you know better than to wrestle Jack Armstrong?

Why, nobody can lick Jack, except Abe Lincoln, of course, and he knows better than to go looking for a fight."

"But they always act so big, coming into town and bragging and all. It makes me so angry that I just had to fight!" he said as he dripped homeward.

"Best learn while you're young that talk is cheap. Stick to your books and you'll come out better in the end," said the man.

So, back in school the next day, the boy took a lot of teasing. Yet, his friends admired him for his bravery and liked him for the pride he had in his town.

Then Mentor Graham rapped on his desk and the school came to order. The teacher was tall and thin and liked to talk more than he liked to smile. Every morning, he walked over from his red brick house and taught the children who were able to come that day. In the winter, the log schoolhouse was quite full of New Salem's children, but with spring fast approaching, more of them were needed at home to get ready for the spring plowing.

This day, even Mentor Graham couldn't get all the mud off his shoes. He studied the floor and he studied our feet, looking for the muddiest pair of shoes, when his eyes rested on Billy's shoeless feet. Still sore from the fight the night before, Billy had not done a very good job of wiping off the mud from his bare feet. There was mud on his heels and mud between his toes. His winter shoes were too small and they hurt too much to wear, even though it was still chilly in the mornings. Mentor Graham and Billy looked up at the same time. Their eyes met. Without saying a word, Billy got up, got the broom, and swept the puncheon floor before he began his studies.

At spelling time, Peggy helped Nancy with her spelling. "Just remember that there is a little word inside the word ORANGE. If you spell RAN in the middle, the other letters will fill in around it."

Nancy carefully wrote the word ORANGE ten times on the slate which the girls shared. Their older sisters, Jane and Ann, had used the slate when they were in school. Someday, baby Sallie would use it too. With nine children in the Rutledge family, sharing was second nature. The boys in the family, David and Robert, shared the other family slate on the boys' side of the room.

The day flew by as each age group in the one-room schoolhouse was called up to read and recite. At arithmetic time, the older children helped the younger ones with their problems, and then Mentor Graham dismissed them with the reminder that there would be a spelling test on Friday.

"I just knew it!" complained Nancy. "Now I'll worry all week about the spelling test and I won't have any fun." But Nancy was wrong about that. She would have fun that week and it was just about to begin.

A shrill whistle blasted the quiet of New Salem village. Distant yelling told the little girls to head for the river. By the time they reached the bluff, they heard another whistle and they could see a steamboat rounding the bend.

"It's the Talisman coming back from Springfield!" cried Peggy.

What Did Lincoln Do in 1832?

A week before, the steamboat had gone upriver, with an army of men clearing the overhanging branches and drifts of logs with long-handled axes and lots of muscles. Now, their friend Abraham Lincoln was guiding the huge boat back up the Sangamon river again to prove that the little river would be good for traveling and trading.

"It's always easy to see Mr. Lincoln in a crowd, isn't it?" asked Peggy. "He's so very tall!"

But there was no time to even shout "Hooray!", because the steamboat was having trouble. The water level had gone down just far enough so that the big steamboat couldn't float over the dam at the gristmill. The men on the boat were yelling at the men at the mill, and the men at the mill were yelling back at them. This went on for some time. The boat couldn't go forwards, nor could it go backwards.

"What are they going to do?" asked Nancy. "If the water goes down any further the boat will be stuck in the mud!"

Then the girls noticed Abraham Lincoln was shouting to his friends at the mill. They didn't seem so mad any more. Just a bit disgusted.

"I'll wager Mr. Lincoln can solve this problem," said Peggy.

And this is what they did. The steamboat men and the mill men worked together and ripped out enough of the dam to let the boat squeeze through, and then they all helped to build the dam back up again.

As the boat sailed down the river to Beardstown, the girls wondered if they would ever see another steamboat on their little Sangamon River again.

"Do you think "steamboat" will be on our spelling test on Friday?" laughed Nancy.

April 1832

Peggy's stomach told her that it would soon be lunchtime. Mother had put two corn meal dodgers and two pieces of bacon in her lunch pail; Nancy had the same. Lunchtime couldn't come soon enough Peggy thought. Her eyes and her mind were not on her ciphers. Much as she loved to learn, she was having trouble concentrating today. The weather was warm, the breeze was rustling the leaves outside the windows and a rather lost bee was buzzing around the room. Nancy's eyes met Peggy's with a look that said, "I can't wait til lunch recess!"

Just then, a rumble was heard in the distance. As it got closer and closer, the children began whispering questions to one another. "What's that noise?" "Is it a drum?" "Can you see what's going on?" Even Mentor Graham became curious and stuck his head out the window.

"It's the New Salem boys marching off to war," he exclaimed. "Class is dismissed for a long lunch hour."

The boys and girls crashed into one another, trying to be the first one out the door.

Peggy, Nancy, and Robert ran up to Main Street and watched the troops with the other cheering folks. Leading the company of soldiers was their friend Billy, the drummer boy! He beamed with pride when he saw his classmates. His legs and arms were still sticking out of his pants legs and jacket sleeves, but he didn't mind—he was excited to be going to fight the Indians in The Black Hawk War. And, he had a new pair of shoes!

The Rutledge children recognized several men in the company. They saw their oldest brother, John, marching next to their brother David. Even though he was only sixteen ("Going on seventeen, Ma, remember!"), David was big for his age and, when he begged his parents to let him go, they gave in. "Stick close to your brother John!" they warned him. And he did. He knew good advice when he heard it.

The children cheered with everyone else as the flag went by, and then Peggy spotted a tall, thin man at the end of the line.

"Mr. Lincoln! Mr. Lincoln!" she called. "It's me, Peggy Rutledge!"

Peggy knew that he couldn't stop and chat with her, and she knew that he couldn't even wave. He was busy marching and carrying his gear. He had on his same old shirt with its sleeves rolled up, and his same old pants that didn't nearly reach the tops of his boots. He even had on his old work hat! When he marched, his long legs looked awkward. But Peggy could see that he was proud to be a soldier.

"Hooray for Mr. Lincoln!" she cried, and she was sure that she saw him smile.

It didn't take long to march up the dusty Main Street of little New Salem, and then the company marched on out of town with the children chasing behind, just like the Pied Piper of Hamelin. The men would march clear to Beardstown to join a group of other men from nearby towns.

Soon the school bell reminded them that they were not soldiers, but students who needed to get back to their studies.

When they were settled again in the log schoolhouse, Robert asked, "Mentor Graham, where are they going and what are they doing?" The question was well-timed and well-asked. Robert knew that such a question required a long answer as only talkative Mentor Graham could devise. And he was right. Mentor Graham wore himself out explaining that Illinois was made a state in 1818 and that a treaty in 1825 had been signed sending all the Indians left in Illinois across the Mississippi River to The West. Most of the Indians had already gone, but old Chief Black Hawk said the treaty wasn't honest and that he wouldn't leave his homeland. Mentor Graham assured the children that the soldiers would chase Black Hawk and the last of the Sauk Indians out of Illinois for good.

Then Mentor Graham went on and on and on about how the land now belonged to the settlers who were building towns and farming the land, until he became quite excited and exhausted. The children never did practice their spelling that day, and they were even dismissed early!

Walking home in the spring sunshine, Nancy reminded Peggy that they had to hurry home and help their mother and big sister tighten the ropes on the beds and air out the feather pillows and mattresses. They loved helping with the spring cleaning. All winter long, their rope trundle bed had been getting looser and looser until the little girls could feel the floor under their straw mattress. They looked forward to sleeping tight again tonight. Soon they were home and could see the pillows and mattresses airing on the fences in the sunlight.

"I'm glad you're home," called Ann. "We need your help."

Nancy reached up on the mantel and got the special turning key. Together, the women of the family pulled on the ropes and twisted the bed key until the beds were tight and good as new. Then they lifted the mattresses off the fence and awkwardly carried them back in the house. They smelled fresh again and the little girls couldn't wait til bedtime to try out their tight bed. So they bounced and giggled while their big sister laughed. If the pillows had been in there, they would have had a pillow fight too, but there was yet work to be done.

The girls had been saving duck and goose feathers all winter, and they had enough to fill two pillows. So, the old feathers were pulled out of the pillow sack, and new ones stuffed in. And, oh, how good that smelled!

That night, their Mother tucked them in like she always did, with baby Sallie in the cradle nearby. But tonight, Mother meant it when she said, "Good night, sleep tight! Don't let the bedbugs bite!"

May 1832

"Are we having mush for supper tonight?" asked Peggy. "We had mush for breakfast and we'll have mush for dinner, so do we have to have mush again for supper?"

"I never want to see mush again!" wailed Nancy.

"I quite agree with you girls," said Mother, "but it's that time of year again. We're in the 6-weeks-want. All the food that we put up last summer is gone, like the beans and apples and potatoes. And it will be a while yet before the new crop is ready to be eaten. The only thing left is corn meal. Just be glad the cow gives plenty of milk or you'd be eating dry biscuits."

"How long will Father and Robert be out at our Concord farm?" asked the girls.

"Well, with John and David still gone to fight the Indians, I expect they will be gone a while. They need to do the work for four men with only two. But they'll be back in town tonight. There's work to be done here too," said Mother.

"That's for sure," complained Nancy. "I'm tired of carrying wood and buckets of water."

"We're going to start planting the kitchen garden today, so when you young girls get home from school, there'll be watering that needs to be done," said Ann. "Hurry right home, you hear?"

Peggy and Nancy heard as they ran out the door of their log house. It was lovely to stroll slowly to school in the warm May sunshine with no shoes and almost no worries.

"If that old Black Hawk War was over, and John and David were back, our worries would be over," said Nancy.

"I doubt it," laughed Peggy. "If they were home, you'd have less to complain about but you'd still find something to worry about! Like the spelling bee on the last day of school!"

"Oh, did you have to remind me?" moaned Nancy. "I still have trouble with words like THERE and THEIR and OUR and HOUR. Why are there two ways to spell the same sound?"

"I'll help you with your spelling again tonight if you help me pick berries for Mother after school," said Peggy.

"But I thought Ann said we had to hurry home and water the garden?" answered Nancy.

"We'll be home in plenty of time to water the seeds. I hope they plant lots of peas and carrots and beans and cabbage and beets... Yum, yum! How I'd like to taste some vegetables right now instead of old mush!" said Peggy. "We'll surprise Mother and Ann with some fresh berries. They'll be so happy to have fresh berries that they won't be mad at all if we are late."

So, after class, the girls headed out of town, hoping to fill their empty lunch pails with berries for them all.

It was still early in the season for berries, so the girls had to wander deeper and farther into the bushes to get the few that they found. Their arms and legs got scratched over and over and pretty soon they started itching. The more they itched, the more they scratched. And the more they scratched, the more they itched.

"Let's go home, Peggy," said Nancy. "I itch all over."

"Let's look a little further," said Peggy. "Our buckets aren't nearly full."

"I'm going home right now!" yelled Nancy. "This was your idea and I think it was a bad one. We're going to be late and itchy and on top of that, we hardly have any berries!"

Peggy reluctantly followed Nancy on the long walk home. The girls were hot, tired, sad and very itchy as they walked with their heads down. They looked up when they heard a horse plodding gently down the road. It was old Granny Spears on her way out of town. Granny spears had been captured and raised by Indians when she was a child, and she knew Indian medicines better than anyone. She was very old and hunched over and her nose and chin very nearly came together, but the children loved her. Why, she had delivered half the babies around New Salem.

They told Granny all about their berry picking mess and she laughed at them while they itched and scratched themselves. Then she reached in her sack and gave them some salve to rub on their scratches.

"Now you get home and help your mama," she advised. And the girls did as she said.

Mother had been worried about them, and she was so happy to see them with only minor scratches that she hardly scolded them at all. They fetched pail after pail of water from the well and carefully watered the rows of seeds. When they finished, they made sure that they latched the garden gate to keep the pigs and cattle out. They knew that a kitchen garden was fair game to the roaming animals!

Father and Robert came home from the farm in time for a plain supper of mush, but with a few berries for dessert. Each and every berry seemed very special because, even though there weren't many of them, the girls had worked hard to provide a special treat.

Soon the last day of school arrived and with it the final spelling bee of the year. Mentor Graham always began with the easiest words first, so the youngest students would have a chance. Peggy could see that Nancy had her fingers crossed when it came to her turn.

Mentor Graham said, "Nancy, your word is ORANGE."

Peggy thought she saw Nancy smile as she spelled, "O-R-A-N-G-E."

Peggy spelled the word OUR correctly, and then missed on CIRCUS. But Nancy stayed in until the very end, missing the word GOVERNMENT. The winner was an older boy who received a satin ribbon.

"Next year I hope I win the satin ribbon," dreamed Nancy.

What Did Lincoln Do in 1832?

And then they were dismissed for the summer. They were free! Free to enjoy long, lazy days of fishing, playing marbles, making dolls, and swimming in the river.

Soon John and David would be home and the family would be together again. As the girls strolled home, they thought there was no place in the whole, wide world finer than New Salem, Illinois.

The Mill

June 1832

It was a sticky, hot day in June. Though it was still morning, sweat was already dripping down Mother's face as she cooked the noon meal in the heat of the hearth. Peggy and Nancy had been sweaty when they woke up, and by the time they got dressed and put away their trundle bed, they too had sweat dripping down their backs.

The little girls kept going in and out of the log house trying to decide if it was cooler inside or outside. They had been to the well and splashed themselves with the cool, clean water twice before Mother had scolded them for being wasteful.

"Put on your bonnets and go out and weed the garden, please," said Mother. "You'll be cooler outside but you mustn't get too much sun on your faces."

Peggy and Nancy were reluctant to work in the sunny garden on such a hot day. But they did as they were told. Mother sweetened the deal by adding that when they were done, they could go swimming in the river.

What Did Lincoln Do in 1832?

"Let's start at the shady end of the row of beans," said Nancy.

"No, let's start at the sunny end, and end at the shady end," argued Peggy. The girls seemed to be disagreeing about everything today.

"You do it your way and I'll do it mine!" insisted Nancy.

In their long calico dresses, bonnets and bare feet, the girls made their way silently down the row, sometimes using the hoe to hack at the weeds and sometimes pulling out the weeds with their bare hands.

"This bonnet is always in my way!" fussed Peggy, as she pulled it off and let it dangle down her back. She was on her hands and knees pulling on a very stubborn weed.

"Mother said to leave it on or you'll get sunburned," Nancy reminded her, like a good, older sister.

"Don't worry, and don't you tell on me!" said Peggy.

The girls should not have said anything to each other because no matter what they said, they argued and fussed. It was just that kind of day. It was so hot, that everything seemed wrong. They knew better than to fuss at Mother, so they fussed at each other. Only the bees seemed to be enjoying the heat. They were happily buzzing from flower to flower, sipping the nectar and pollinating the plants. The girls ignored the bees, knowing that with all the flowers around, the bees were not going to bother with them.

What Peggy didn't know, was that one bee had flown into her bonnet which was still hanging down her back.

"Put your bonnet back on, or I'll tell," said Nancy once again.

"Oh, all right," answered Peggy and she tugged her bonnet back into place.

The trapped bee could only do one thing to protect itself, and before Peggy could figure out what was wrong, the bee stung her in the back of her neck.

"Oh, oh, oh!" screamed Peggy as she swatted at her neck and tried to pull her bonnet off. "I've got a bee in my bonnet!"

She threw her bonnet on the ground and ran into the house. Mother quickly saw the problem and pulled the stinger out. Then she laid a cool, wet cloth on Peggy's neck and one on her forehead and sat her down in a rocking chair. By the time Mother applied some of Granny Spear's salve for insect bites on the red lump, Peggy had stopped crying. A hiccup every once in a while was the only sound she made as she rocked away the hurt.

For their noon meal, Mother had made a soup out of early spring vegetables, like cabbage and onions, with corn meal dodgers on the side. Father, John, David and Robert all came in from the mill to eat. It was good having John and David back from the War, and the family was all together again. The guests of the inn had been fed first, and now the family sat down to eat, rest and talk about the day's activities.

Father was saying that they were very busy down at the mill. So many boys on horseback had brought bags of meal to be ground, that there was a long line of horses standing nose-to-tail on the hill. But the boys were no where to be seen. They had all headed down into the river for a swim.

"If Mr. Lincoln were here, I reckon he could help you at the mill," said Peggy. She was a bit put out that Abraham had not returned from the Black Hawk War with John and David. She missed the way Mr. Lincoln talked to her like she was important and grown up.

"Well, he'll be coming home soon, you'll see. When our time was up, he enlisted again. I guess he was having such a good time fighting the mosquitoes that he wasn't finished being a soldier yet!" laughed John.

"I hope he gets to fight real Indians," said Peggy. "He's so strong, I'll wager he could lick them all!"

"I think he just wants to chase them out of Illinois, not fight them. Why one day, an old Indian wandered into our camp, and the men all wanted to kill him right then and there. But Captain Lincoln, he said that if they were gonna kill that old Indian, they'd have to fight him first. And nobody dared do that! So, the Indian just wandered away again," said David.

Peggy tried to understand. If the Indians were so bad, why didn't Captain Lincoln kill him? And if the Indians were good, why was there a war against them? She promised herself that she'd ask Abraham about that when he returned.

Then it was time for Father and the boys to go back to the mill and it was time for Mother and the girls to clean up the house and do their afternoon sewing work. But in no time at all, Mother was saying that it would be OK if the little girls went swimming down in the river.

Peggy and Nancy hopped, skipped, and jumped their way down to the creek. At the mill, they could see the long line of horses with their heavy loads, waiting patiently in the shade of the tall trees. They could also hear the laughter and the yelling of the boys still enjoying their afternoon swim. As the girls got closer, the boys got real quiet. Something was up. The girls knew that the boys were planning to splash them, and send them running away. But not these girls! They hadn't grown up with three big brothers and learned nothing! To the boys' surprise, the girls stripped off their dresses and plunged into the cool water with their underwear on! And when the boys tried to splash them, the girls splashed right back until they all decided it would be more fun to play something else.

All afternoon, the children swam, caught frogs, made rocks skip waves and laughed and giggled. Then one of the boys got out a rope and tied it to an overhanging tree branch. They took turns swinging on the rope and letting go way out in the middle of the river. They measured who landed the farthest out and cheered for the winner.

One by one, the boys had to leave as their corn was ground into cornmeal and it was time for their long rides home. Peggy and Nancy dried off on a rock, then put their dresses back on and slowly walked home, thinking that nothing was finer than hot summer days on the Illinois prairie.

July 1832

All the whoopin, and hollerin' out on Main Street told Peggy and Nancy that something was happening.

"Can we go see, Mother, please?" asked Peggy.

"All right, but stay nearby, don't go wandering off," said Mother. "There's work to be done." Then with a twinkle in her eye she added, "But if it's something big, come back and get me!" Mother was a good sport. She remembered her own childhood days and the excitement of something unusual amidst the routine.

Down on Main Street, the men were gathering to watch a horse race. These horse races were usually the result of a bragging argument as to whose horse was faster. The argument had begun in the grocery where whiskey was purchased and drunk, and now the men had spilled out onto the street and the horses were being lined up. The winner would win nothing but bragging rights but that was pretty important.

The horses came galloping down the street, but Peggy's eyes were no longer on the sweating mares. She was intently watching a tall figure, who was just entering Main Street at the west end. The race ended, and all attention was on the winner; but Peggy was running the other way to welcome home her friend, Abraham Lincoln.

"Mr. Lincoln, Mr. Lincoln, you're home!" she cried.

"You're a sight for sore eyes, Peggy Rutledge!" he replied.

At dinner that night, Abraham told the family of his three months in the Black Hawk War. He told how his duty ended 'way up in Wisconsin Territory. Since someone had stolen his horse, he had to walk most of the way home. From Peoria to Havana he had paddled a canoe, and for a bit he had shared a horse, but most of the way, he had walked.

The conversation turned to Abraham's plans for the future. Father had encouraged him to run for the state legislature, and that vote was coming up soon. Abraham felt his long absence would hurt his chances, but said he'd still give it a try.

Then Father said something about John McNeil, the man whom Ann was engaged to marry. Peggy didn't catch it all, but she understood enough to know that John was going away to see his parents for a while, and that Father had bought some land from him at Sandridge.

"Are we fixin' to move, Father?" asked little Peggy.

Everyone got real quiet and Father slowly answered.

"I told you last February that our family liked to move around a bit. Seems to me, we've had a good time here in New Salem, but

I've got a hankerin' to live on a farm again. Maybe we should move in the fall before winter storms set in." No one else said much. Even Abraham looked down at his plate and dinner ended quickly.

The next day, Peggy finished her chores and asked her Mother if she could go for a walk. Mother could see that something was troubling her, so she gave her permission to go. Peggy set out to find Mr. Lincoln. If she could find him, he would be sure to have answers to some of her questions. This business of moving had really confused her.

Her path took her west on Main Street, past Mr. Hill's store; past the hatmaker who was boiling up a foul-smelling brew of wool, fur and the chemical mercury to make felt hats; and past the cooper's shop, where he was busy making barrels. Peggy kept her eyes peeled for Mr. Lincoln, until she spotted him sitting under a tree with Mr. Kelso, deep in conversation. They each had a book that they were studying, and every once in a while, they read something out loud to each other.

Mr. Kelso was reading something from a book by someone named Shakespeare. Peggy didn't know what it meant and she thought the words sounded peculiar, but Abraham seemed to enjoy listening to Mr. Kelso's loud, booming voice. Then Mr. Lincoln quoted a poem by someone named Robert Burns. Abraham's voice was kind of squeaky, but Peggy liked the sweet way he recited the lines.

Then Peggy spoke up. "Mr. Lincoln, why does it hurt my heart so much to think about moving?"

Abraham said he thought this would be a good time to go fishing. He and Peggy walked down to the creek in a comfortable silence. Peggy knew that he would take her question seriously and not make fun of her.

They sat with their poles in the muddy water for a long while. When Abraham finally spoke, Peggy listened. He told how sometimes on a summer evening, when the air was very still, he could feel the earth breathing,[1] and hear the corn growing and see the stars moving across the black night sky. He told how by growing, things changed. But by not growing, life ended. Peggy understood that this also applied to her. As she grew, things would change in her life too. And somehow, in the gentle way he said it, Peggy took comfort in knowing that change came to all who truly lived. Somehow, moving didn't seem quite so scary anymore.

When Peggy got home that afternoon, Mother asked her if everything was all right.

"Oh, yes, mother," said Peggy. "You'll see. Everything will be all right. You don't need to be afraid of moving and changing." Mother smiled a loving smile.

A few days later, Peggy noticed a crowd gathering in front of Mr. Hill's store. She wandered over to see what was going on.

Mr. Lincoln was getting ready to give a speech. He stood up on the porch with his hands in his pockets, and began:

"Fellow Citizens, I presume you know who I am. I am humble Abraham Lincoln. I have been solicited by many friends to become a candidate for the Legislature. My politics are short and sweet, like the old woman's dance. I am in favor of the national bank. I am in favor of the internal improvement system and a high protective tariff. These are my sentiments and political principles. If elected, I shall be thankful; if not it will all be the same."[2]

Lincoln practiced giving that speech to his friends in New Salem. They didn't care if he was tall and skinny; they didn't care if he was poor; they didn't care that his clothes didn't fit him; they cared only that he spoke the truth in plain words they could understand.

Peggy cared too. She had a feeling that she wasn't the only one who was going to grow and make changes. She had a feeling that Abraham Lincoln was growing and changing too.

August 1832

Voting Day was August 6, 1832. The men of the town of New Salem lined up outside the voting place, usually a store, and waited their turn to go in and vote. Inside, a clerk and a recorder wrote down the votes as each man stood in front of their table and announced in a loud voice (viva voce) for whom they were casting their vote. Since most men in the New Salem area could not read, voting out loud was the natural way to vote.

That day, almost every one of the men in New Salem voted for Abraham Lincoln (277 out of 300). But the people of the surrounding area who did not know of him, voted for others. So, in his first election, Abraham Lincoln lost. He had said that if he lost "… it would all be the same …" But when Peggy Rutledge saw Mr. Lincoln that evening, she knew that it wasn't all the same. She knew that he was disappointed and wondering what life held for him next.

What Did Lincoln Do in 1832?

Peggy didn't have much time to worry about Mr. Lincoln though, because her family, and many other families in town, were getting ready to spend a week out on the Rutledge farm in Concord at a camp-meeting. Peggy looked forward to this exciting week each year. She knew that at these church revival meetings, there would be preaching and singing, and eating and playing.

It took careful planning and lots of packing to load the wagon for the trip out to the farm. Father was a leader of the Cumberland Presbyterians in the area, so he liked to get out to the campgrounds early and get things organized. There was a large shed for the preaching already out there, but everything else had to be hauled out in the wagon. Mother spent many days getting the tents, bedding, cooking utensils and food together. She knew from past experience that she would spend most of her time cooking for the many people who would attend.

The camp-meeting officially began on Sunday, but the Rutledges headed out on Thursday to ready the area. On their way down Main Street, Peggy saw Mr. Lincoln walking along with a book under his arm and asked him if he was coming out.

"I may come out for one day next week," he said," but Mr. Berry and I are now the proud owners of our own store, and I have lots of work to do here."

"Maybe if you do more workin' and less readin', you and Mr. Berry would both have time to come out to the camp-meeting!" teased Ann.

"You know me too well," Abraham laughed as he strolled along.

The Rutledges were the only ones camping out the first night, but by Friday, others were arriving to help get ready.

To make a cooking fire for the women, two huge logs were hauled behind the shed, and these helped steady two Y-shaped iron rods, one at each end. Another smaller iron rod was laid across the Y from which the women could hang their cooking pots.

By Sunday, the camp looked like a little village. With the shed as the center of activity, tents fanned out in all directions, with wagons and horses and cows nestled comfortably in the shade of the old trees.

When the church services began, the preacher's loud voice was heard everywhere, inside and outside the shed. He read from the Bible and raised his voice against the sins of the world (especially the sins of the men of New Salem who tended to drink too much whiskey!) When he prayed, his voice fell to the softest whisper, causing the believers to lean forward in their seats, straining to hear. Then, his voice rose with great emotion, and as he slammed his fist on the table with a loud bang, the people literally jumped in their seats. All this enthusiasm kept the folks interested for hours on end.

Peggy's favorite time came when the preacher taught the folks a new song. She'd come running from wherever she was and screech to a halt in the front row as the preacher lined out the song. Since there were no hymn books, and very few people could read anyway, he began by singing a line of the song, directing with his right hand to indicate if the tune should go up or go down.

This year, 1832, the preacher was lining a song from his new copy of <u>Virginia Harmony</u> called "Amazing Grace". All Peggy needed to hear was the first line,

> *"Amazing grace, how sweet the sound,"*

and she knew that she would love the new song the rest of her life.

The preacher's hand rose as he lined out the second line,

> *"that saved a wretch like me!"*

The next two lines spoke to her soul,

> *"I once was lost, but now am found,*
> *Was blind but now I see."*

Peggy hummed that tune the rest of the week, making up her own words and verses when she couldn't recall the real words.

It seemed the only ones not having fun at the camp-meeting were the women who were stuck cooking all the food for three meals a day for all the folks. They cooked and baked in the humid August air, trying to overhear the singing and preaching in the shed. The hardest part of their job seemed to be to keep all the dogs away from the food. People had brought so many dogs out to the camp with them that it was not unusual to see a dozen dogs hovering close to the food, awaiting their chance to snatch bits away.

Peggy got it into her head that it would be fun (and helpful too) to shoo the dogs away. She looked around and found a grove of walnut trees, dropping green walnuts to the ground. She gathered some in her apron and returned to the fire. She found that if she threw a walnut with all her might, and if her aim was true, a dog would yelp and run away.

Now, the women approved of this behavior, as they thought the dogs a big nuisance. But one dog owner came to complain when he saw what she was doing. Peggy bravely told him that if had left his dogs at home this wouldn't be a problem! He walked away and never said another word about it.

As the week ended, the intensity of the preaching increased and many people "got religion". This happened in several ways. Some folks got baptized; some fainted; some were healed; and some would get the "shakes" like poor Mrs. Johnson, who set to shaking so hard, she had to be taken home and put to bed for several days!

When the week was finally over, the Rutledge family packed their wagon and headed home. Father looked pleased with the work of religion, Mother looked exhausted, and Peggy looked back over her shoulder and wondered if they would be moving out to the farm permanently, come fall.

The Berry-Lincoln Store

September 1832

William Berry and Abraham Lincoln had bought an "old stock of goods, upon credit" and joined several others who tried to make a living by storekeeping in New Salem. Their old stock of goods came from another storekeeper who had been unsuccessful, given up and moved on. Since there already were a few successful stores in town, some doing a big business in whiskey, and some doing well by shipping up the latest goods from St. Louis through Beardstown to New Salem, the new shop found it difficult to compete.

Lincoln had recently returned to New Salem after three months in the Black Hawk War. He had lost the election to the state legislature, but was "anxious to remain with his friends who had treated him with so much generosity". Actually, he had no where else to go.

So, when Peggy peeked in the Berry-Lincoln store one day in September, and asked what they were doing, "taking inventory" was the answer. She watched as they counted the candles and mixing bowls and bolts of cloth that they had to sell. They had coffee, sugar, salt and a barrel of flour. And they had a glass jar on the counter with hard candy inside.

But the most important thing they had was their friendly, honest reputation. People in town recalled how Abraham had once walked a great distance to return just a few pennies to someone he had accidentally overcharged when he was the clerk in Mr. Offut's store. People called greetings to them from the street, and stopped by just to chat. Sometimes, they talked about books they read, and sometimes they talked about politics. Abraham seemed especially fond of talking about politics.

Peggy watched as Mrs. Burner stopped in to buy some flour. Mrs. Burner had no money that day, but Mr. Lincoln just wrote down what she bought and let her have it on credit. He treated her with the same respect that he treated the people who had money.

The next customer traded a dozen eggs for a gallon of molasses. Trading and buying on credit were not unusual ways of doing business in the small towns sprouting up in the Old Northwest. Money was hard to come by, but hope was plentiful.

Mr. Lincoln saw Peggy eyeing the candy, and winked as he gave her one. "One candy to celebrate the opening of our new store," he said.

With September came the start of a new school year. Mentor Graham ran a subscription school, and charged the children a few pennies a day. This month, only Nancy, Peggy and little William would be going to school. David and Robert were needed to work on the farm, at least until October.

On the first day of classes, Mother reminded the girls to give Mentor Graham his pay and to keep an eye on William. The girls promised, and dutifully held his hands on the walk to school.

William was assigned to sit on the lowest log bench with the other beginners. Nancy and Peggy were still seated on the middle log.

"I hope next year I get to sit on the top log," whispered Nancy.

"Then you wouldn't get to sit by me anymore!" Peggy whispered back.

"That might not be all bad!" teased Nancy.

Just then, Mentor Graham looked up and saw who was doing the whispering. He walked over to the children with his switch in his hand.

"I hope the Rutledge girls don't start off the year with a black mark for whispering instead of working!" he scolded.

The girls blushed red to their ears, and then heard William in the front row hissing, "Ooh! I'm telling!"

"And you, young man, will learn on the very first day of school that you will not be a tattle-tale!" said Mentor Graham to William in his loud voice.

William was surprised and scared, but he did his best not to cry. "How could I be in trouble already?" he wondered.

Nancy and Peggy were learning multiplication this year, and while the other children did their work, the children of the middle bench were standing and reciting out loud:

"Twice one is two, this book is very new. Twice two are four, let's trace it on the floor. Twice three are six, we're always playing tricks. Twice four are eight, the boys are always late. Twice five are ten, let's do it once again."

Then Mentor Graham asked the back row to stand, and drilled them on the history questions they had been studying:

"What is the capital of Illinois?" he asked.

"Vandalia," they said in unison.

"Who is our president?" he asked.

"Andrew Jackson," they answered.

"And how many stars are in our flag?" he asked.

"Um..." the children in the back row looked to each other for help.

"24," whispered Nancy over her shoulder.

"24," the children proudly replied.

At lunch, the children took their lunch pails outside and sat under the trees to eat.

"How did you know that there are 24 stars on the flag?" Peggy asked her big sister.

"I guess I've been listening to everyone's lessons for so many years, that I know many things that might surprise you!" she replied proudly.

Then the boys played marbles and the girls played jacks until it was time to go in again.

In the heat of the afternoon, Peggy noticed William's head nodding until it fell on his chest. The little boy was all tuckered out.

The children laughed as he woke up with a start when Mentor Graham put his hand on his shoulder.

"There will be no black mark for falling asleep on the first day of school, William, but make sure it doesn't happen again tomorrow," said the teacher kindly.

On the way home that day, William was glad that the children had agreed that they would not tattle-tale on each other.

October 1832

"Girls, run up to Mr. Hill's store and see if there is a letter for us today," said Mother. "I'm expecting to hear from our relations in South Carolina any day now. And get our newspaper while you're there."

"We'll go right away," said Peggy, who was always glad for an excuse to put down her sewing. She knew that Mother didn't like going to the postmaster, because the post office was in the store where he sold whiskey as well as other goods. The ladies in the town of New Salem didn't like the way Mr. Hill made them wait for their mail while he served the men in the back of the store who were buying whiskey. Mother complained over and over again that New Salem needed a new postmaster.

"Someone with better manners," she'd say.

But the girls didn't care if he made them wait a bit. That gave them more time to look around and talk to the interesting folks who made up the little town on the Sangamon river. Today, they were excited to see their friend Mr. Kelso hauling a deer skin through the doorway.

"Ooh! Can I feel it, Mr. Kelso?" asked Peggy politely.

"Sure thing, little Peggy," he said as he smiled at her.

She reached out her hand to touch the skin, feeling how soft it felt if you rubbed down on it, and how rough it felt if you rubbed up on it. She especially liked the little white tail that it ended with.

"Would you like to feel it, too?" Mr. Kelso asked Nancy.

"No, sir! Not me! Are you eating her for supper tonight?" she asked with her hands safely clasped behind her back.

"No, Nancy, we're not having HER for supper tonight, we're having HIM for supper tonight!" laughed Mr. Kelso and the other men. "This is the skin from a buck, and speaking of bucks, Mr. Hill, why don't you hand me a dollar for this here skin?"

"Here's a buck for a buck, Jack, and you bring in some more skins like this any time," said Mr. Hill.

Then he handed Nancy and Peggy their mail and received their postage money in return. Then he went to the back of the store with the other men.

At home, Mother wiped her hands and sat right down to read the letter. Her family described their doings, and Mother set to daydreaming and wishing that her old home weren't so far away.

Peggy understood how her mother felt. The talk of moving just a little ways still made her feel a mite low. What if they moved far, far away from New Salem?

After school the next day, Peggy walked down Main Street so she could pass by the Berry-Lincoln store. Mother had told her she must not be a beggar, and Peggy promised herself that she wouldn't accept candy from Mr. Lincoln even if he gave it to her!

She saw him lying in the shade of the tree in front of the store, reading a book.

"What are you reading, Abraham Lincoln?" she called to him.

"I'm not readin', I'm studyin'," he said with a grin.

"Oh. Well, what are you studyin' then?" she asked.

"Surveying," he declared. "It's like measuring. Here, you stand over here, and hold real still."

He handed her one end of a grapevine which he unrolled as he walked away. He explained how he could measure a piece of land that someone wanted to buy, so that they would get their money's worth. He put a stake in the ground and carefully measured a 90 degree angle for a corner.

"There," he said. "That's one corner of the property owned by Miss Peggy Rutledge."

As he rolled up the grapevine again, Peggy noticed that it was getting dark already. Every day, it was dark a bit earlier than the day before.

"The days sure are getting shorter," she said. "I wish it could be summer all the time, but I remember what you said about the whole earth growing and changing, just like me." Then she paused and said, "If we move out to the farm soon, will you still come visit us?"

"You couldn't keep me away!" he said with a smile.

Peggy got home about the same time as her father and brothers. They had spent their day at the saw mill, and still had wood shavings on their heads, on their clothes and on their shoes. They stood outside and brushed each other off, just as they would brush snow off each other in the winter months to come.

Mother had venison stew cooking in the big, black kettle hanging over the roaring fire. Biscuits were steaming on the table, and the boarders were already eating. A second table had been set up in the bedroom for the family to eat upon, and everyone sat down to a hearty supper.

The garden had provided them well this year. There was fresh corn to eat and plenty to put away for winter. There were pumpkins and squash on the vine, apples on the trees, and potatoes and carrots to be dug from the ground.

After supper, Mother got out the big scissors and pieces of clothes that were worn out and started cutting shapes.

"What are you going to make, Mother?" asked Peggy.

"It will be a new quilt," said Mother. "A quilt is for remembering, and this quilt will always help us remember the friends we've made here in New Salem."

While the girls watched, Mother carefully cut squares and rectangles of different pieces of fabric. She arranged them carefully until Peggy could make out the shape of their log house.

"It's our house, Mother, The Rutledge Inn!" squealed Peggy. "There are the two front doors, and the window and the chimney!"

"What other houses can you make, Mother?" asked Nancy. "Can you make one to look like Mr. Onstot's house and cooper shop? Can you make one to look like our schoolhouse? Can you make one to look like the mill by the river?"

"And can you even make one that looks like the store that Mr. Lincoln and Mr. Berry just bought?" asked Peggy.

"Slow down and give me enough time, and I think I can make a quilt of our whole little town. It's so small that I reckon' it will all fit easily on a bed quilt," said Mother.

Peggy never tired of watching her mother work on the New Salem quilt. As Mother sewed, the family told stories of the people who lived in the houses that she was piecing together.

It would take months to sew the top and more months to quilt the whole thing; but it would bring years of pleasant memories to generations of Rutledge family members who would sleep under the log cabin quilt, and dream of the days when they lived at New Salem.

The Kelso-Miller House

November 1832

The presidential election of 1832 took place on November 5. The men of the New Salem precinct voted at Sam Hill's store with Abraham Lincoln and his friend William Green serving as clerks. Lincoln waited until everyone else had voted, then he voted last. Andrew Jackson won his bid for re-election by a wide margin. In New Salem, two-thirds of the men had voted for Jackson, the first president to have been born in a log cabin. But Abraham Lincoln had voted for a fellow Kentucky man, Mr. Henry Clay, who lost.

The next day, Peggy Rutledge saw Abraham Lincoln heading out of town on a horse with a book in his hand.

"Where you heading, Mr. Lincoln?" she asked.

"To Springfield with the election returns, Miss Peggy. I'll be back in a couple days," he replied.

Peggy knew how much Lincoln liked to take those long rides into Springfield. He had lots of time to read as he slowly rode along, and once in the city, he had lots of people to talk with. Maybe he'd even meet someone who would loan him another book!

When Mr. Lincoln returned to New Salem, Peggy was waiting with BIG news. Her father had sold their house to Nelson Alley, and their plans for moving to their farm north of Concord were in full swing. They would be leaving as soon as they could get ready.

Although the news was expected, both Peggy and Mr. Lincoln looked a bit down in the mouth. They knew that they would still see each other, but it would never be as easy as it had been living in the same town.

They were distracted by Mr. Kelso, who happened by at just the right time.

"We're fixin' to build us a new log house, Lincoln," he said. "Would you be willin' to lend a hand for a day or two? We sure could use your strength and long arms to our advantage!"

"Be pleased to oblige," answered Abraham. Everyone in town knew that they could count on Lincoln to help out with whatever needed to be done. Why, he'd helped build the dam, raise houses, split rails for fences and chased runaway horses! When strength was required, he was always there, ready to help.

"See you early tomorrow, then," said Jack Kelso.

Peggy was up and dressed early the next morning. She never wanted to miss out on any fun or excitement, and a house-raising promised to be both.

Mr. Kelso was fixin' to build on the far west end of New Salem. He had smoothed the dirt where the house would be, and the men were measuring and setting out the flat stones for the corners.

But instead of four stones for four corners, Peggy counted eight stones for eight corners! What a big house this was going to be! She couldn't imagine why Mr. and Mrs. Kelso would need such a big place for just the two of them.

Just then Abraham Lincoln came over and saw the question in her eye. He explained that this would be a DOUBLE house, with a kind of a porch between them. The other house would be for the Miller family with their children. Then Peggy remembered that the Kelsos and Millers had been living together in a very crowded, hastily put up log cabin. The women were sisters and they liked living close together, but not in the very same cabin! It was time to build nicer log houses, sharing a friendly porch between them.

Good straight trees had already been chopped down and were laying on the ground close by. Two sides had been trimmed with an adze, so that they were about six inches wide. Their ends had already been notched with an axe so that they would hook together.

Neighbors were turning out to help. Everyone liked Jack Kelso, and everyone was eager to help build this unusual double house. It started to feel like a party, with the men hoisting logs; the women getting fires going to cook the food to feed all the people; and children running around getting in the way in their efforts at being helpful.

Opposite walls were started by placing the first long logs on the stone corners. Next, the other shorter walls were started by placing two shorter logs upon the ends of the first logs, hooking them in place by their notches. Two long, two short. Two long, two short. Little by little, the log walls went up. They made kind of a game of it, with the men building the Kelso side trying to stay ahead of the men building the Miller side.

Peggy and the other children cheered for everyone. They even cheered for the women who were doing the cooking. The day ended with not one but two log houses raised with their roof poles in place. Of course the light from the setting sun shone right through the house in the gaps between the logs, as the tired folks sat in the grass to eat their thank-you meal.

The second day, about half as many folks were there to climb the roof and cover it with shingles. A cold, light rain was falling, reminding them all that winter was on its way and that the work needed to be done quickly and well.

Some folks were still there on the third day to "chink" the walls. Small pieces of wood splits were squeezed in the spaces between the logs. These helped to fill the spaces but didn't quite do the job completely. So the last part of "chinking" was to plaster the cracks with a mixture of mud and cattle hair. The men forced the mud between the logs and smoothed what oozed out.

Peggy heard some noise coming from inside the new cabin, and soon she saw Mr. Kelso's jolly face peeking out the new window at her! She waved and laughed as she watched him adjust into place a sliding window he had invented.

The double-house had taken most of a week to build, and there was still more to be done to make it complete, inside and out, but the two families could now move in. A wagon pulled up and they unloaded their things into the two houses. A great many laughs were heard as they tried to decide what furniture would go into which house! The shared porch would make a wonderful place to eat together in fine weather; and it was comforting to know that help and a friendly ear were right next door.

When Mother got out her quilting work the next time, Peggy asked, "Do you still have room for a double house on the quilt, Mother?"

Mother laughed as she said, "Consider it done."

The Blacksmith

December 1832

Clang! Clang! Clang! Clang!

A new sound echoed through the town of New Salem in the quiet of the early morning. Peggy laid in bed and tried to wake up. She had been dreaming of moving again, and this time, the horses pulling their wagon made a loud clanging noise every time they put down their hooves. But as she yawned and opened her eyes, the clanging noise continued. It wasn't a dream.

Peggy woke Nancy saying," What's that noise? Do you know?"

Nancy was wide awake immediately. "No, I don't know what it is, but let's get dressed and go find out."

So they did. The girls dressed for cold weather. They pulled on wool stockings, and flannel petticoats under their dresses.

As the girls came into the kitchen, Mother was serving breakfast to the boarders. Today, there was a slice of ham with their corn meal biscuits and hot coffee.

"Good morning," Peggy said politely to each of the men. "What's the clanging outside? Do you know what it is?"

"That would be the sound of Mr. Miller, the blacksmith. I believe his shop is finished, and he's already doing business," said one of the local men. "This town sure needed a blacksmith. Now we can have iron door hinges, and our horses can get good shoes right here in town."

The girls ate their breakfast mush, and helped Mother clean up. Then, they asked for permission to stop at the blacksmith's shop on the way to school.

"Of course you may go. But don't pester Mr. Miller with a lot of questions. He has work to do and you need to get to school!" laughed Mother.

The day was bright and sunny, but chilly. The girls could tell that winter was truly on the way. They walked quickly down Main street, skipping and twirling as they went. The doors and windows of stores and houses were all closed to keep the warmth of the fireplace in and the cold of the winter wind out.

The town almost seemed unfriendly. There were no people walking about, no cheerful "hello" from an open door, and no children playing in the yards. Winter was not Peggy's favorite time of year.

The closer that they came to the shop, the louder the clanging became. Every once in a while, it stopped and it seemed that the whole town held its breath awaiting the next clang. Then, when it came, they all could go on breathing again.

A bright glow shone out from the window and from the open door of the blacksmith's shop. The huge, hot fire in the forge kept the shop so warm, that even on a cold day like today, his door stood ajar.

"Oh!" squealed Peggy. "The blacksmith's door is open. He must want us to come inside. Doesn't it look warm and cozy?"

Nancy had to agree. It did look bright and inviting. Others must have agreed with them, because two men were already inside, sitting on barrels and watching and visiting with Mr. Miller while he worked.

"Hello there, girls," called Abraham Lincoln between clangs. "Have you come to see what the noise is all about?"

"Yes," they chorused. They tried to time their words between swings of the blacksmith's mighty hammer. With each swing, the girls braced themselves for another clang, yet they jumped each time, to the great amusement of the men.

Then, hissing sounds and billowing steam arose from a bucket of water, as Mr. Miller cooled a hot piece of iron. In the quiet that followed, Peggy asked what he was making.

"Right now I'm fixin' to make a proper lock for a door, so Mr. Onstot can lock up his cooper shop," he said. "Then I'm gonna shoe Mr. Watson's horse. While I'm working, I'm gonna set Mr. Lincoln straight on a few things too."

Abraham laughed out loud. Mr. Kelso and Mr. Miller laughed too. Anyone could tell that they were good friends who enjoyed good-natured teasing. Today, Abraham had another book with him. When Peggy asked, Mr. Lincoln told her it was a book about law. He read from the page he was on, and all three men gave their opinions as to what the law meant and how it could be applied.

"Seems like you are always studying on something new, Mr. Lincoln," said Peggy.

Abraham reminded her that when he was little, he hardly ever was able to go to school, and had only a book or two to read. Now, he was trying to make up for lost time.

"Speaking of lost time, isn't it about time for you girls to be getting to school?" he asked.

"We'd better run the rest of the way," urged Nancy.

But as she left, Peggy lingered in the glow of the bright fireplace and the warm circle of friendship. It reminded her of something, but she couldn't quite remember what.

The days of December flew by. Father talked about when would be the best time to move to their farm up on the Sand Ridge; and Mother tried to think about things to be moved while she cooked and sewed, as usual.

Then one day, it dawned on Peggy that Christmas was almost there. Mother seemed busier than ever, and once, when Peggy saw a package in the cupboard, Mother quickly closed the door and told her not to ask any questions.

On Christmas Eve, Mother sat plucking the feathers out of a big goose, and Ann was carefully counting out candle stubs. She made sure that there was one for each of them to carry to church early on Christmas morning. When it was time for bed, the little children were allowed to hang one of their stockings on the fireplace mantel.

It was always hard to sleep on Christmas Eve, but before Peggy knew it, Mother was waking them up in the darkness of early morning. In their stockings, the children found a candy treat and a pair of mittens Mother had made especially for them.

After a little breakfast, the family bundled up and joined other families who were walking to Christmas services in the schoolhouse. As they entered the schoolhouse door, they each lit their candle and found a place to sit. Wide-eyed Peggy looked around at the faces of her friends and family, glowing in the warm light from the candle flames. And then she remembered! The warmth and happiness she had felt in the blacksmith's shop had reminded her of the warmth and happiness she felt here in church on Christmas morning.

The preacher read the Bible story of Jesus being born in Bethlehem, and they sang carols that filled the room with sounds of joy and peace.

Peggy looked around at her New Salem friends, and tried to fill herself with the glow of their love. When she blew out her candle on the way home, she held her breath, and yes! She could still feel their love deep inside. She knew she could carry that love with her wherever her life took her, as she grew and changed, just like the earth, and just like her friend, Abraham Lincoln.

The James Rutledge Family

James Rutledge married Mary Ann Miller, January 25, 1808. Their children included:

Jane	Born 23 November 1808
	Married James Berry February 28, 1828
	Died 1866
John	Born 29 November 1810
	Married Sarah C. Harris May 26, 1854
	Died 1879
Anna	Born 7 January 1813
	Died August 25, 1835 at farm near Concord
David	Born 22 August 1815
	Married Elizabeth Sims December 24, 1840
	Died 1842
Robert	Born 25 February 1819
	Married Sarah Plasket January 8, 1845
	Then married Samantha Jenkins,
	November 1, 1848
	Died 1881
Nancy	Born 10 February 1821
	Married Anthony Prewitt. October 14, 1846
	Died 1901
Margaret	Born 21 June 1823
	(Peggy) Died 1864
William	Born 29 November 1826
	Married Olive C Bennett April 18, 1852
	Died 1917
Mary	Born 5 June 1827
	Died 23 July 1827
Sarah	Born 20 October 1829
	(Sallie) Married John P. Saunders 1852
	Died 1922

Notes:

1. From the musical, ABRAHAM! by Ken Bradbury and Robert Crowe, 1979.
2. Abraham Lincoln, <u>The Collected Works of Abraham Lincoln</u>, ed. Roy P. Basler et al., 9 vols. (New Brunswick, N.J.: Rutgers, University Press, 1953-1955), 4: 60-67.

Additional References:

<u>The New Salem Tradition</u>., Lincoln's New Salem State Park, Illinois Department of Conservation, January, 1984.

Pratt, Harry Edward, <u>Lincoln Day by Day</u>, The Abraham Lincoln Association, Springfield, Illinois, 1941

Reep, Thomas P., <u>Lincoln at New Salem</u>, (Petersburg: old Salem Lincoln League, 1927).

The Rutledge Family Bible, Museum collection, New Salem State Park.

Thomas, Benjamin P., <u>Lincoln's New Salem</u>, (Springfield: The Abraham Lincoln Association, 1934)

What Did Lincoln Do in 1842?

Betty Carlson Kay

January 1842

Today I start a new chapter in my life. I'm commencin' to be a writer! And it's all on account of my new friend, Mr. Abraham Lincoln. I can't quite figure how it happens that he fancies talking to a skinny, twelve-year-old school boy like me, but he says he gets more pleasure out of wilin' away the hours with me than he does with anybody else jest now. Settin' 'round the fire at the back of the Ellis store gets mighty lonesome, says Mr. Lincoln, now that his best friend, Joshua Speed, has headed off to Kentucky to get married. BUT SHUCKS! What's so pleasurable about *my* company, him being a real grown-up lawyer and all. Why he's even got a tailor-made suit and a stovepipe hat that makes him look to be the tallest man on earth. I bet I never get me nothin' as fine as that.

Back to my writin'. Mr. Lincoln says that when somebody wants to recall something important, he's got to write it down. So that's what I'm fixin' to do right in this here book he made me. Yup, he folded up some paper and kind of sewed it up the side and announced, "Here you go, Jed, you're a writer now too!"

I said, "Blank paper don't make no writer out of a boy like me." But he just shook his head and said, "Jed, you just put down on paper the words you think in your head and you'll be a writer."

I pressed him for more help. "If you was to write something down right now, what might you say?"

"Well just now, I'd probably say that I'm the saddest, most miserable creature on earth. [1] But I've got good friends, like a boy here named Jed, who can still make me laugh over nothing."

My mama's good manners reminded me not to pester a grown-up man about his miseries. Besides, everybody here in Springfield, Illinois knew Mr. Lincoln was the gloomiest giant that ever walked the wooden sidewalks around the new capitol. Long-faced, and stoop-shouldered, he was seen at all hours of the day and night, in rain, sleet and snow, sometimes mumbling to hisself. Somethin' about a lady named Miss Mary Todd and a broken engagement. Wouldn't you jest know it'd be about a girl?

We stared into the firelight in a silence so deep, somethin' had to change. After a bit, he told me he reckoned it was a good night to practice my oratory. So he opened his book of Aesop's fables and told me to read one of his particular favorites, the one about a lion and some bulls.

The Lion and the Three Bulls

For a long time three bulls pastured together. A hungry lion lay in ambush in the hope of making them his prey, but was afraid to attack them while they kept together. Having at last by guileful speeches succeeded in separating them, he attacked them without fear as they fed alone, and feasted on them one by one at his own leisure. The moral:
"A Kingdom Divided Cannot Stand"

I struggled to read it out loud and when I was done he said now read it again and say each word clearly. After three times, he finally clapped his huge hands together and said, now go write it in your book. He reckons the best way to recollect something is to read it over and over and then to write it down.[2]

When I was fixin' to leave, he watched me put on my layers which I pretend keep me warm on these blustery cold January days, and that awful sadness filled his whole body when he saw that my shirt was so thin it only had one side. Then he noticed the several inches of skin betwixt my pants and my boots.

"You're as hard to keep covered as I was at your age," he mumbled, and for just a bit, he smiled. Then he was lost again in that far away look he gets.

February 1842

I was feeling a mite down about my readin' and writin', but mostly I was sick and tired of winter, when I trudged my way into the backroom of Mr. Ellis's store for a bit late one Saturday afternoon in February. I was bettin' I could find Mr. Lincoln there, or at Billy's barbershop, and sure enough, he was settin' there with one book in his hand and a pile of books on the floor.

After running errands for folks all day, it would seem I had near as much mud on my boots as there was on the roads around town, and I stomped off a good deal of it before I slopped up his floors worse than they already were. But Mr. Lincoln, he just leaned way back in his chair and set his long legs high up on the stovepipe and said with a smile, "That reminds me of a story about the mud here in Springfield, Jed."

"One day a mild mannered gentleman came into the Hall of Representatives and asked permission to speak. The Secretary of State asked him what he wanted to speak about. The man said, "The second coming of our Lord." "It's no use,"said Mr. Campbell, "don't waste your time in *this* city. It is my private opinion that if the Lord has been in Springfield once, he will not come a *second* time!"

As he laughed at his own joke, he went on, "Never you mind now Jed, the wind's changing direction and by morning, the muddy mess will be frozen solid again. Old man winter can't seem to decide if he should stay or go on his way."

"If I had my druthers, he'd be long gone by now," I said. "But some folks can't seem to get enough of the snow and cold. I hear talk about some pretty gals getting up one last sleigh party out to Rochester. Maybe you should be fixin' to go with them."

He gave me half a smile and said, "That's mighty kind of you, Jed, but I'd be feeling alone whether I went with them or I stayed here. So I best work on my speech for the Washington Society."

Now I well knew how that Washington Temperance Society felt about the poor folks who visited drinkin' establishments, and how superior they felt about being teetotalers.

Mr. Lincoln noticed my face flush beet red. I couldn't look him in the eye, so I just sat and stared at the glowing coals. And Mr. Lincoln, he could tell I needed some time to gather my thoughts before I spoke, so he just set there with me, like he had all the time in the world. Finally, the words kind of tumbled out on top of each other. "It jest ain't fair the way they say all drinkers are worthless dregs of society. Why, they jest don't know how it really is!"

Mr. Lincoln looked at me with his heart in those sad eyes of his and gently said, "Tell me how it really is, then, Jed."

And so I did. I told him how hard my father works, hauling stuff for people all day in his wagon, and how sometimes the old wagon breaks down, and his deliveries are late and people say insulting things to him and how he needs a drink to make hisself feel better again, and how we never have enough money to get all the food and supplies we need and how me and my sisters and brothers don't have but one slate between us for school and how some kids laugh at us when we have to share, and how I'm trying to work and help out but then I can't get my learnin' done neither.

Well, he let me pour all that out without stopping me once til finally I was done. Then he quietly says, "Always bear in mind that your own resolution to succeed is more important than any other one thing." [3]

We set a spell longer while our own memories spilled all over us, till I pulled on my wolf-skin cap and said I had to be going. I thought that was the last of it, but I was jest readin' in this week's Sangamo Journal, the words Mr. Lincoln said in his big speech on the 22nd to the Washington Temperance Society. Seems like he made a lot of people mad 'cause they wanted him to preach loud and long about how low the people are who drink to excess, and how high and mighty are the folk who don't drink. Instead, he quietly said, "... such of us who have never fallen victims have been spared more by the absence of appetite than from any mental or moral superiority over those who have."[4]

I wonder who he was thinkin' about when he said them words.

March 1842

Such screeching and wailing as you never heard echoes across the prairie when the new Northern Cross Railroad comes to town! Why, you can hear it way up on Jefferson Street in the old part of Springfield where my family lives. Soon as I hear that chuggin' I head myself over to the 10th Street station to watch the excitement.

Folks always have tales to tell of their rail journey from Jacksonville or even all the way from the Illinois River. Seems like there's always something going wrong, and the passengers have to pitch in and help the crew or they'd be stuck out on the prairie til kingdom comes. Like the time they ran out of firewood and everyone had to get off and hike to the tree line to gather logs and branches and drag them back to burn in the firebox. Or like the time they ran out of water for the boilers and the passengers took turns toting heavy bucketfuls from a stream about a mile yonder. Sometimes they arrive here lookin' as tired and bedraggled and dirty as they do getting off the stagecoach at The Globe after a 25 hour ride from Chicago.

But they always set off lookin' fresh and eager. Why jest the other day, some ladies and gents rode the train to Jacksonville jest to meet up with their friends who live over there, and have

What Did Lincoln Do in 1842?

a party. 'Course, it weren't anybody lives by me. No sir. These downtown aristocrats have the time and the money to go all the way to Jacksonville jest to party! They had their own band to make them all jolly too. Yup, the drum was beating and the horns was blaring and the ladies was giggling and waving their hankies. Whew! Such a great to-do. One of the ladies was Miss Mary Todd whom Mr. Lincoln once courted. That was before his big sadness took him over. Well, when I reported to him that I'd seen her looking so gay, he said, "God be praised for that." [5]

Then, like one party wasn't enough for them, don't ya know, a couple days later, the Jacksonville folks rode the train to Springfield, and they all had another party together in The American House. Ain't no tellin' what rich folks'll do next.

Mr. Lincoln, well, he's not a partaker in frivolity nowadays. He's busy up in his new law office across the street from his old office at #4 Hoffman's Row. Seems like he's busier than ever, now that he's partners with Mr. Stephen T. Logan. Used to be he was partners with John Todd Stuart, a pal from when they was soldiers in the Black Hawk War. When Mr. Lincoln decided to partner up with Mr. Logan, all he had to do was gather up a few books and papers and march himself across the street to Mr. Logan's office. Mr. Lincoln chuckles and says it's an advantage being poor because you ain't got much to tote when you remove yourself from one place to another.

So now Mr. Lincoln's got more cases than ever to study, and this Mr. Logan is teaching him to prepare them in a goodly manner. In fact, Mr. Logan says to study and plan like you was the lawyer for the other side; then you can fix the argument for your own side more firmly in your mind.

All this takes a considerable amount of hours and I often times catch up with Mr. Lincoln walking to the Capitol building where there's a library full of law books. We walk together in the north door, and part company. Then I take my time before I exit the south door. If I'm lucky, I may see somebody real important like the Governor, or I might overhear a judge sounding high and mighty in the Supreme Court. If I have lots of time, I tiptoe upstairs and have a seat in the visitor's gallery of the House of Representatives. No one's there right now, but a year ago, I seen Mr. Lincoln standing tall and addressing the House on matters of great importance to the State of Illinois, like more railroads and fixin' our bank system. Mr. Lincoln's been a legislator four terms, since 1834, but now he's expecting not to stand for election again. So I asked him if he's gonna stand for the United States Congress next time, and he replied, "Never you mind now, Jed, but if you should hear any one say I don't want to go to Congress, I wish you would tell him you have reason to believe he is mistaken." [6]

When I told Mr. Lincoln that I fancied being a lawyer too someday, he said, let's start by studying on your ~~spellin'~~ spelling. Starting now.

April 1842

Chicken Row is my favorite block in Springfield, 'cause I can't never be sure what I'm gonna see there. The buildings are kind of lopsided and it don't seem like nobody cares if the awning is droopy and half falling down. For sure I'm gonna see chickens there; some squawking with a rope tied around one foot, and some with their necks rung and still oozin' blood into the dust. And if I'm really lucky, there might be a chicken head staring up with a surprised eye still trying to figure out what just happened to her. A passel of cats then have a hissy fit over who saw it first. Gutted rabbits and squirrels do a right fine job of attracting more than their share of black flies.

So, I was headed west on Washington Street, enjoying the aroma and confusion on Chicken Row, when I noticed a familiar figure strolling ahead of me. Mr. Lincoln has a peculiar way of walking, like as if his body can't quite get used to being attached to such long legs. He stoops forward a bit, so as to make his stove pipe hat lean forward, instead of pointing straight up to heaven. He was coming out of Billy the barber's shop looking freshly shaved and trimmed. I told him he looked a sight better than when I'd seen him last and he laughed and said ain't nobody can make him look anything but a sight. Well, peculiar as he looks on the outside, he's for certain the best person I know on the inside.

He bought us each a sarsparilla and invited me to set a spell with him in the back room of the Ellis store. He said he'd be leaving me in charge of Springfield for a bit, as he was setting off to ride the Circuit in the morning. While this seemed to cheer him up considerably, it kinda brought me down. But seeing as how he'd been so low for so many months, I tried my best to be happy for him too.

"So what's it mean to ride the Circuit, anyway?" I asked.

He told me then about folks who live way out on the prairie, far from towns and legal help. Sometimes those folks get to feuding about whose hog is whose, or whose land is whose or even whose money is whose. So a judge and some lawyers ride from small town to smaller town trying to straighten out the fussing. They stay about a week in each town, holding court. It takes about ten weeks each spring and about 10 weeks each fall to ride the whole circuit.

It got me to thinking about if I'd like to be the kind of lawyer what rides the circuit. So I said, "What's the fun in that?"

And Mr. Lincoln, he gulps down the last of his sarsparilla and commences to draw me a word picture of the fun on the circuit.

"Firstly," he said, "there's the kind of fun I reckon you're meaning. The kind of fun can't help but happen when a gang of like-minded men gathers anywhere. Some nights, there's the kind of jawin' that goes on around this here fireplace. Many a yarn is spun; many an idea is contemplated; and many a friendship made. Likely as not, the whiskey gets passed and someone will start to bragging and before you know it, there's a foot race or a wrestling match out on the street. Or, if we're real lucky, there might be a play or a lecture in town of an evening."

"Secondly, there's the kind of fun that's from winning in the courtroom. So often times I study in the evening. When I have a particular case in hand, I love to dig up the question by the roots and hold it up and dry it before the fires of my mind."

Now, I admit to liking to learn something new, but reading's awful hard work at times, and then I start to thinkin' maybe I'm just not smart enough to be a lawyer and all. But Mr. Lincoln, he just says, "Never you mind now, Jed. It'll all come out right in the wash."

May 1842

Spring fever spread like prairie fire this week, and my friends and I planned out a little adventure. So, Friday night, long about midnight, I was upstairs reading with one eye, while listening for their signal with two ears. When I finally heard the whistle, I was out the attic window and down the honeysuckle vine before you could say George Washington.

The full moon shone down on us and lit our way as we headed out Jefferson to Spring Creek. Our plan was simple. We was fixin' to take a swim and be home again before we was missed. But best laid plans have a way of turning out the worst way.

We stripped down and whooped it up as we ducked and splashed each other in the shallow creek. But a rustlin' in the reeds was a dead give away that we wasn't entirely alone. We reckoned we'd find whoever was spyin' on us and teach them a lesson. So naked as jay birds, we scrambled up the bank on the far side. It was right easy to follow the culprit, what with the bright moonlight and the commotion he made. We cornered him betwixt some fallen logs and were right surprised to find it weren't no person spying on us at all. The white stripe down the critter's back gave it away. It was a big old pole cat, staring at us with shining yellow eyes.

My friends expected a lot out of me:

"Dare you to touch his nose, Jed."

"A nickel says you can't grab his tail, Jed!"

With my friends' encouragement, I reckoned I could accomplish the both with my daring and quick wit. Before I could give it a clearer thought, I grabbed for the little stinker. I was fast, but the skunk was faster. Instead of catching the skunk, I caught a peck of trouble. Sure as shootin', that dern skunk soaked me with a most vile spray, from my head to my toes. Whoopin' and a-hollerin', I dove back in the creek and done my best to remove the offending odors.

There weren't nothin' I could do except trudge home, expecting a good hiding in the morning. And I weren't far from wrong. The worst part weren't my mother's scolding nor her hickory switch. Nope, the worst part was the tub full of a foul-smelling mixture of berries and vinegar that I had to soak in. Yuck! I even had to wash my hair in it. And I still stunk.

Just when I thought nothin' good would come of the whole live long day, a surprise note from Mr. Lincoln put a smile on my face. It said,

> "Dear Jed,
> You asked me about riding the circuit in our last conversation, so I am writing to tell you that last night, while riding to DeWitt County, we lawyers slept 10 in an attic room fit for two or three. [7] Judge Davis, owing to his 300 pound bulk, was allowed to sleep

alone. The rest of us doubled up. Such snoring and hacking and coughing could have woken the saints. The one towel afforded us was too soaked to do my face any good when it was my turn to wash up in the morning. But, the better part of one's life consists of his friendships, [8] as these made on the circuit.
Your friend,

A. Lincoln

Makes me think that sleeping in the attic with my brothers ain't such a bad arrangement after all. Maybe I'll have to think again about being a circuit riding lawyer.

June 1842

I better get to writing this down so I'll always remember the hoopla last week when former President Martin Van Buren came to Springfield. Since he only just recently lost the election to be President of the United States for a second time, it seemed he needed a bit of cheering up.

Some folks here in the capital city couldn't wait for the important man to arrive, so they trekked a mile out east on the Rochester Road to escort him in proper like. The Springfield Band was tooting; the Sangamon Guards were marching; carriages was rolling and folks was hiking, just so they could all meet up with him and yell theirselves hoarse. Why, I even seen Billy the Barber marching with the Springfield Artillery, dressed to beat the band in his blue suit with bright red cuffs, collar and big old red plumes on their helmets. He was blowing away on his clarinet, with his flute tucked in his pocket, should he need it.

Me? I just went along to see what there was to see. Mr. Lincoln joined up with the crowd but he made himself scarce, seeing as how he's a Whig and Mr. Van Buren is a Democrat. They don't exactly see eye to eye on how to fix the money problems facing the United States banks just now, so Mr. Lincoln left most of the excitement to others.

When the parade arrived in town, the Springfield Artillery fired a thirteen gun salute to rouse the citizens further. Some of us thought this didn't spook the horses quite enough so we hustled around and found ourselves some fireworks. By settin' them off in strategic times and places, we undertook to put a panic in every horse's eye, a twitch in every tail and a cussin' in every rider. We also saw to it that some boring speeches were made a bit more exciting.

Most of the afternoon, the famous Mr. Van Buren let folks come visit with him at The American House on Adams Street where he was staying. I ran errands for a few folks and had a couple coins jingling in my pocket while watching the comings and goings of some important folks, and some others who only thought they was important.

Round about supper time, I was fixin' to head home when I recalled that my mother needed me to stop at Mr. Bunn's store for some loaf sugar. His grocery on Adams Street, right across from the capitol building, is a sight to behold. He don't have just a little bit of everything like the other stores, why, he's got a whole *lot* of everything stacked floor to ceiling. I reckon if he doesn't have what you need, you don't really need it much. And toward the back, Mr. Jacob Bunn's got himself the blackest, heaviest iron safe in town. And what with folks not trusting the state banks these days, they're commencin' to keep what little cash they have in his big, old safe.

Mr. Lincoln says if he ever had enough money to fret about, he'd be likely to do the same, as a more trustworthy man than Mr. Bunn can't be found. But Mr. Lincoln has his own "national debt"[9] to worry him. Ever since his store in New Salem "winked out"[10], Lincoln has been slowly and faithfully repaying his half of the debts they owed. And since his old partner William Berry had died, he'd been repaying Berry's half too. Mr. Lincoln reckoned it was the honest thing to do.

By evening, I was back at The American House watching the comings and goings of Springfield's aristocracy. They was fixin' to attend the ball, done up in honor of Mr. Van Buren. Folks must've been sprucing themselves up for hours. The ladies especially in their shiny dresses all tied up with ribbons and laces; and the gents looking and smelling better than I'd seen them in months. Odds were good for the single gals, as there were about ten beaux for each of 'em. I reckon their feet hurt the next day from all the dancing.

I fell to sleep that night planning how I'd look in a few years, waltzing with every pretty girl at the ball. But in my dreams, the pretty gals turned into huge skunks who stunk to high heaven. Guess I'm not quite ready for such fancy affairs.

July 1842

Parched. That's my new favorite word for July. Just like my throat. It's more than hot. It's more than dry. It's more than windy. It's all of them together that makes it so miserable. The clouds done forgot how to gather themselves up and do their business. Ain't nobody complaining about the muddy streets no longer. Now there's cracks in the road deep enough to snap a wheel right off a wagon. I won't even write about the dust, whew.

It's too hot to be outside in the daytime, and too hot to be inside in the nighttime. My whole family sleeps on the porch as do the neighbors. The creek would be the place to be except the water's all but gone. They say even the Sangamon River is dry clear to New Salem.

We did get the tiniest bit of rain one morning when me and my friends were out hunting. The mourning doves took time to perch on the split rail fence and catch as many drops as they could. We laughed when the silly critters lifted their wings up high, first the left one, then the right, like they was trying to wash their underarms. They commenced to set there so long, like they was just waitin' for us to shoot them, so we did. We got two which ain't more than a mouthful. Then we set our sights on bigger game. My mama would've been right happy with a rabbit or two, but, like she says, patience ain't our long suit, and we come home empty handed.

Since it were Saturday, there was lots of goings on in town. Wagons were in from every part of the county, loading up with supplies and what have you. Families spent the day visiting with friends they ain't seen for a while. I reckon it gets a mite lonely out there on the prairie, and folks need to commiserate with others when they can. The whiskey always flows free like, when folks is gathered and before long, don't you know, there was a horse race on, just for the bragging rights. It would make the Sunday headache much more pleasant, if you was the winner of a Saturday race.

But this horse race weren't like any I'd ever seen before. The boys up from Sand Ridge challenged the Clary's Grove boys and before I knew what was happening, they was fixin' to tie a big old gander by his feet on a branch of the biggest oak tree around. Helpless, the squawking bird had no notion of what was in store for him, and I didn't either. After covering the poor bird with grease, one of the Sand Ridge boys rode hell bent for leather and reached up to pull the head off the silly bird. All's he got was a handful of grease. Then a Clary's Grove boy raced down the street, and got a better hold but still came away without the prized head. By this time, I was hopin' the old gander was dead enough not to even know what was happening to him. The boys commenced with fussin' about somebody puttin' too much grease on the old bird's head. And the gander, he was jest dangling there. When the Sand Ridge boys succeeded in finally pulling the head off, the Clary boys set to blacking every eye near by.

Me? I didn't reckon I needed to stick around. I knew the trouble that could erupt when the heat and the whiskey were mixed together. I went down the street hoping I'd run into Mr. Lincoln. Then I saw him coming out of the house of the editor of the paper,

Mr. Simeon Francis. He had a funny look on his face, like he was happy and a mite dazed at the same time.

I couldn't wait to tell him all about the gander pulling. But the more I talked about it, the less I liked thinking about what had just happened. Seemed almost as mean as puttin' hot coals on a turtle shell, just to watch the naked critter squeeze itself out.

Mr. Lincoln's smile disappeared as I talked and then he said, "Jed, I reckon the boys meant no harm. But I recall when I was about your age, I shot a turkey with my father's rifle more by accident than skill.[11] I promised then and there I'd never harm another living thing. I reckon you feel the same."

I do. I swear here and now, I'll never hurt another helpless critter. Guess I'll have to do a lot of fishing 'cause somehow that don't really seem like killin'.

August 1842

August 15

There's something happening here. What it is ain't exactly clear. But I aim to find out. First of all, Mr. Lincoln's been disappearing. Then, when I do see him, he's strolling along and smiling out loud. Why, I even heard him whistling as he headed up the street toward the Francis house on 6th Street. When I asked him where he was goin', all he said was "Never you mind now, Jed."

There's been many a coming and going at the Francis house lately. I ain't been spying, but I do my share of noticing. It ain't meddling 'cause I ain't said a word to nobody but I have noticed that round about the time Mr. Lincoln pays an afternoon call on Mrs. Francis, two young ladies are also paying a call on her. One gal is Miss Julia Jayne, whose pa is the doctor a few blocks from my house on Jefferson Street. The other I believe to be the very same Miss Mary Todd that Mr. Lincoln was fixin' to wed before the time of his big sadness. If they keep this up, I'll be forced to take action.

August 18

Curiosity got the best of me and I found out that grown-ups sure take a fair amount of pleasure from the most unlikely activities. Now I seen what's been going on and, golly, it ain't worth nothin' at all.

See, the other day I tiptoed a fer piece behind Mr. Lincoln as he walked to the Francis house. After him and the ladies were all safely gathered inside, I quietly drug a barrel to the parlor window and slowly peeked my head up over the sill. There they set at the fancy table meant for playing games. But were they playing cards? No! Were they playing charades? No! They was writing! Reading and writing and writing and reading! Through the open window I heard the dainty laughs of the young ladies echoed by the booming guffaws that only Mr. Lincoln makes. I couldn't make out more than a few words of what they was saying, but I swear I heard them talking about *Aunt Rebecca*.[12] So, who's she?

But what got me was the way Mr. Lincoln was looking at Miss Todd. Fact of the matter is, it appeared that Miss Todd was doing all the talking and Mr. Lincoln was eying her like a devoted pup.

I would've stayed longer but the heat of the afternoon brewed up a right fine mess of lightning, and some bolts was gettin' a mite close to my perch on the keg. If only the lightning would be accompanied by rain, but no such luck. Great bolts split the sky at the same moment the thunder roared, meaning only one thing: they was too close for comfort what with me standing beneath the tallest trees around.

In my roundabout way I started heading for home through all the fireworks when one particular bolt struck the lightning rod atop the house of Mr. Forquer. For a second, it appeared to be a decoration on the rooftop, and then the sparkle fizzled down a wire and blackened the dry grass where it met the ground. Seemed to be a right smart way to keep your house from catching on fire.

Too bad there ain't such a thing as a lightning rod for corn fields, 'cause before I reached home, I could smell danger a-comin' our way. Smoke from several prairie fires was blowing east as the winds picked up. Before I knew it, I could see the orange fire licks racing across the black sky and I knew the fear of being surrounded. Now, a prairie fire fanned by gusty winds is so fast it can outrun a man on horseback. And it was heading smack dab toward Springfield.

The fire was already nudging the log cabins and frame houses on Washington and Jefferson when I got there. Folks were heaving buckets of water on their rooftops, and beating out sparks with wet rags, neighbor helping neighbor, til the skies opened up and pelted us with huge drops of rain. Then there commenced a great whoopin' and shoutin' and praise bein' while we kicked up our heels in a wild and wooly rain dance.

Next day, the corn crop weren't nothin' but charred stalks and folks was still as poor as ever; but life would go on and the prairie would give us its greatest gift- the chance to try again.

September 1842

Mr. Lincoln always says to write down whatever it is that a body wants to recall, so I will write down what's been happening lately, 'cause this is really a week to remember.

It all started after school on Tuesday when I was hanging around the corner of 6th and Adams. Mr. Elijah Iles' American House is usually a good place to hear the latest gossip, and that day was no exception. The crowd setting in front of the hotel was complaining about the gosh awful heat that was stinking up the manure piles and the outhouses. Even the "gentlemen" were sweating and they were just setting there in the shade. They should try running errands for a day or two, then they'd really be sweating.

Soon the complaining commenced to speculating. When they mentioned the name *Lincoln* in the same breath as the word *arrested*, I most nearly dropped my dipper of water. Now my big ears serve me very well and without appearing to be rudely listening in, I could hear most everything they said. Something about a duel being illegal in the state of Illinois and the sheriff thinking about putting the two men in jail til they could cool their tempers which were hotter than the current heat wave.

Then one of them said he'd seen Lincoln riding west on the Jacksonville Road early that very morning. "What's he going there for?" I knew I was butting in on the adult conversation, but I just had to know!

"Well, if you must know, he went to buy broadswords for the duel. Then he plans to keep riding til he gets to Alton where he can cross the Mississippi River into Missouri where dueling is legal," said one of the gents.

"But what are they dueling about? Mr. Lincoln would never fight in a duel, would he?" I was so excited I asked two questions in one breath. But by then the men were thinking I was asking too many bothersome questions and they told me to take myself somewhere else. Which I did. I ain't dumb. I knew where I could get even more information.

I headed due west on Adams Street, past the capitol building to the alehouse near the Globe Tavern. Chances were good I could gather even more news, by finding someone who had been enjoying some liquid refreshment on such a hot afternoon.

Again I was in luck. No sooner did I arrive red-faced and out of breath than I ran into a fella settin' on the bench who was willing to tell me a long confusing tale of the affairs that had started with some letters Mr. Lincoln had written to the newspaper.

"You mean the Sangamo Journal?" I asked.

"That's the very one that printed the anonymous letters the past few weeks," said he.

"But if they were anonymous, then they weren't signed by Mr. Lincoln, so how do they know who wrote them?" I pestered.

What Did Lincoln Do in 1842?

"Well, this other man, Mr. Shields went straight to Mr. Francis, the editor, and demanded to know who wrote such slander of him," he answered.

"I can't believe Mr. Lincoln would ever write something so bad that there had to be a duel over it. What exactly did he write?" I hoped he'd keep up his end of the conversation til I knew the answers to all my questions.

"Well, kid, you know how the state paper money here in Illinois ain't worth nothin' these days? Now this Mr. Shields, he's the state auditor, and he says the money can't even be used to pay taxes! Yup, the state printed the money and now nobody can use it and no one has silver money either so folks are afraid that they will lose their farms if they can't pay their taxes."

"So Lincoln complained that the paper money's no good. Everybody knows that. It ain't worth fighting a duel over."

"Well, this Mr. Lincoln got to writing about more than just the paper money. He got to teasing a bit about how Mr. Shields was a ladies man and all, and the teasing got to ridiculing and now Mr. Shields says his honor is at stake."

Well, that was Tuesday. I got copies of the old Sangamo Journals and read the offending paragraphs. Was I surprised when I saw they were signed "Aunt Rebecca". (Was this the same *Aunt Rebecca* I overheard Miss Mary Todd and Miss Julia Jayne and Mr. Lincoln laughing about a while back?)

Now, I know people write stuff in the paper all the time and don't sign their real names, but most everyone suspects who the writer is. Sometimes several people write the letter together, but this time, Mr. Lincoln insists it was just him.[13] Usually it don't mean nothin', they're jest politicking. But this time I guess the teasing went too far 'cause it was about ladies and gents and flirtin' and all.

So anyway, by Thursday, Mr. Lincoln and this Mr. Shields and their seconds got all the way to the Mississippi River and crossed over to an island on the Missouri side. Off came their coats and up went their sleeves. They were taking some practice swings with the huge broadswords when some more folks from Springfield showed up and everyone tried to settle the fuss without somebody getting hurt. (I can guess who'd be hurt, and at 6-feet- four- inches tall and holding a huge sword, it wouldn't be Mr. Lincoln!)

Well, don't you know, pretty soon they all settle their grievances, and shake hands, and even tell each other jokes on the long ride home to Springfield. I tell you, grown ups ain't nothin' more than big kids most of the time.[14]

October 1842

People sure come and go quickly these days. Take Mr. Lincoln, for one. He's off riding Old Buck on the fall circuit, but on Saturday nights, he's back in Springfield. Never done that before. He strides in, linen duster flapping, and strides out again with no time to gather his old friends 'round the fireplace to spin a yarn. Wonder what the attraction is? Sure enough ain't me!

Oh well, right now, I'm busier than ever. Ma's feeling a mite poorly, and she's depending on me to do the chores, run the errands, and see to the little ones. That is, when I'm not at school or running errands for paying customers. I've got it fixed in my head to get to school every day. No playing hookey for me for a while. My reading and writing are improving, just like Mr. Lincoln said they would.

Besides all that, the whole town is buzzing because the Circus and Menagerie are expected any day now! I'm earning me some quarters so I can see with my own eyes the wonders they are advertising in their bills, like animals we ain't seen on this prairie since the last time the circus dragged itself way out west. I hope they are hauling a lion this time.

I've been working a tad extra for Mr. Francis, who lives right next door to his paper. He's all head up over his garden these days, so on Saturdays and Sundays I grab a shovel and see what's needing done. He's forever putting in new starts and moving old plants to new places where there's better light or more room. The nuisance hogs running free all over town ruin everybody else's garden except for his because he's growing a real live fence! Yup, he brought some starts of Osage Orange up from Oklahoma a few years back, and planted them where a fence would be. Now they've grown to be horse high, bull strong and pig tight. If it weren't for that, the hogs would trample down all his other plants like they do elsewheres. Seems like a right smart idea, and looks good too.

October 5

The circus arrived yesterday and the headmaster was as anxious as us youngsters to see what was to be seen, so he dismissed school early. Fancy wagons and dazzling performers paraded in the street while the calliope filled the air with exciting tunes. When time came for the performance, I had enough money for me and my whole family to take our seats way up front. The spangled gal riding bareback at full speed around the ring fairly took our breath away. But when she stood up and rode at that breakneck speed, we all stood up and cheered ourselves hoarse. Then the showman hung an 18 foot anaconda snake 'round his shoulders and brought it by real close for folks to see, and the festive cheering commenced to panicked screaming and crying and hollering. Near us, the huge black snake licked its forked tongue out too close for comfort. Folks scrambling to get away knocked over chairs and one corner of the tent. When the snake was safely back in its iron cage, the show continued to a right smaller audience. Next morning, the circus dragged itself out of town, and we calmed ourselves back down to our usual state.

  The circus excitement sure put some color back in ma's cheeks, but it didn't last long. While reading the paper the other day, I got me a new idea. There in bold letters was an add for a new-fangled tonic, Peter's Pills, guaranteed to perk a body up and put the pink back in their cheeks.[15] It was now available at Wallace and Diller Drug Store, so I hurried myself over to see how much it cost. My quarters left over from the circus didn't quite stretch to pay for the pills, but Dr. Wallace said I could be trusted to pay him the rest next week. When I proudly delivered the goods to my ma, she smiled and said she'd save them for later, 'cause right now she had the kind of ailment that took care of itself in a few months. It took me a while but I soon figured out that we was to have another baby coming our way. Not that I don't like babies, but I wish that money was as easy to come by as a new brother or sister.

On Sunday, after church, I trudged back over to Mr. Francis's house to see if I could earn a few more quarters. Now I owed Doctor Wallace for the medicine, and money would be even more scarce at home soon. I could hear ladies' voices inside the house and pretty soon, don't you know, here comes Mr. Lincoln quietly tiptoeing up the front steps. I gathered I had just figured out why Mr. Lincoln was coming home weekends from the circuit. Seems to me a long way to travel just to take tea with the ladies, even if one of them is Miss Mary Todd.

November 1842

Well I'll be a blue-nosed gopher. Mr. Lincoln wed Miss Todd on Friday night. It all happened so fast that even Miss Todd's sister, Mrs. Elizabeth Edwards was surprised and they live together in the same house! Suddenly, on Friday morning, Mrs. Edwards had a heap to do. There was not enough time for Watson's to prepare their special pyramid of macaroons,[16] so Mrs. Edwards had to make do with other goodies. Good thing she has the help of some Negro servants, what with two little children underfoot.

Since I looked to be the right size and shape, I was sent running several errands for her after school. But, for Mr. Lincoln's wedding, I reckon I'd do anything I could to be helpful.

First, I went and put a few things on the Edwards' account at Mr. Bunn's store:[17]

#6 almonds	1.50
1 jar prunes	1.00
1 gal wine vinegar	.50
1 mackerel	.25
1 qt. sperm oil	.50
	$ 3.75

When I delivered the parcel to the kitchen girl, I sneaked a peek at the front parlor. It smelled of furniture polish and lamp oil, and looked right fine to me. Elegant is a good word for such finery. It brought to mind the fancy reception room at The American House Hotel, without the Turkish splendor.

Then I carried a note to Reverend Dresser at the Episcopal church saying the wedding that night would be at the Edwards' mansion, not at his home. Mrs. Edwards insisted that her younger sister be married the proper way, from the family home on the hill, just like another sister, Frances, did. Miss Todd was fixing to wear the very same dress and pearl necklace her sister had worn too.

Then long about seven o'clock, I held the reins for Mr. Lincoln when he arrived in his plain black buggy, looking pale as a ghost. He kept fidgeting with his tie and running his fingers through his hair which further inclined it to stick out in all directions. He patted my shoulder in thanks, sucked in a deep breath and headed up the front steps. He glanced back only once, and seeing my downhearted face, he said, "Never you mind now, Jed. We'll still be friends."

What Did Lincoln Do in 1842?

Now, Mr. and Mrs. Abraham Lincoln are beginning their married life in one small room on the second floor in the Globe Tavern. Fact is, it's about the same size (8'x14') as the log cabins he was raised in so long ago. "I sure haven't come up very far in this world," was all he said about that. It's the exact same room Mrs. Lincoln's sister Frances lived in for three years when she first married Dr. Wallace. For four dollars a week, they got a room upstairs, with meals in the dining room downstairs. But it must be a mite noisy what with the blacksmith right next door, and the bell clanging every time a stage pulls up.

It's not near so fine as The American House, but not near as costly neither. That's good for Mr. Lincoln who don't ever seem to have much money, and rarely does he seem to care one wit about his constant shortage of funds. But Miss Todd, I mean Mrs. Lincoln, is accustomed to aristocratic niceties, like large rooms and polished silver. So she must really fancy him, as she had plenty of other suitors. I hear tell she always said she was fixing to marry a man who would become the President of the United States.[18] Now don't that just beat all? Does she really think that Mr. Lincoln will be elected President some day? I can't quite imagine him as Mr. President because I don't think they let you put your feet up on the stove and tell stories when you're in charge of the whole United States of America. And I know Mr. Lincoln won't never stop telling stories.

On my way to school early on Monday morning, here comes Mr. Lincoln riding in his buggy, heading out of town.[19] The circuit was still in session, and he was leaving me in charge of town again.

This time, he was also leaving me in charge of Mrs. Lincoln. He dropped some coins in my hand, and said to make sure she got her paper with the mail this week, as she loved to keep up with the goings on in the world.

So, though some things appear to be just the same as always, I have a feeling in the pit of my stomach that things will never be quite the same between myself and my friend Mr. Lincoln.

December 1842

I think I'm dying, was what I said to Mr. Lincoln one snowy day in December, when I'd caught up with him at Billy's. I'd learned that when I needed to find Mr. Lincoln and he wasn't in his office with Mr. Logan, nor in the Supreme Court room in the capitol building, there was a mighty good chance I'd find him in the back of the barbershop. Seems like Billy's is the favorite meeting place for Mr. Lincoln and his cronies, especially with Joshua Speed gone. A shave from Billy beat a shave at home most days, as he served up news and opinions with every customer. Being that Billy was a free Negro, as he hailed from "Hayti", he had a unique way of looking at the goings-on in town. Why, when he arrived in Springfield back in '32, and noticed the lack of a catholic church, he fixed up his own parlor and had a priest say a mass right then and there! He bought and sold property hither and yon, and when he needed a lawyer, why, Lincoln was his man. Seems like Mr. Lincoln counted Billy's opinion just like the other men's, even if his skin was almost as dark as coffee.

What Did Lincoln Do in 1842?

Mr. Lincoln looked up quickly from his ever present book, and said to tell him all about it.

So I did. I told him how my legs ache, and how they sometimes twitch when I least expect it. He asked if the pain ever caused me to lie awake at night, and when I said yes, he said, "I was just like that at your age."

"You mean I'm not dying?" I asked. After he reassured me that I wasn't, he told me how his legs used to ache when he was fixing to have a growth spurt. He said how he grew 4 inches one year, and how the aching nigh on to killed him. Especially at night. I said he must've had several sleepless nights before he got to the height he is now. He laughed and said he reckoned that was true.

Then he looked serious and asked if I ever felt so tired that I thought I'd just keel over. He said he used to get in a passel of trouble for being slow to chop wood and kill snakes and haul water to his log cabin. Since he was so big and strong, seems folks thought he was shirking his duty and just being plumb lazy. He said he started to believe them til his growing stopped and his energy returned. When I told him how angry my father gets at me, he said his father did too. He added that his father taught him to work, but he never taught him to love it. A good book always did more for him than hard laboring did. Then he said to come with him and he'd prove how valuable his book learning has turned out to be.

I followed him across the street to the capitol building, and he invited me to come set a spell and watch the proceedings in the Illinois Supreme Court. I chose a bench half way back, so I could see and hear everything clearly without being in anybody's way.

The wintry afternoon brought little light through the glass panes, so the clerk set about taking fresh candles out of their wooden boxes up on the wall, and fixing them in their stands. Velvet curtains made the courtroom grand indeed. No shenanigans would be allowed in here. No sir. The judge and the lawyers were all business, and even Mr. Lincoln seemed intent on being serious. Not like the circuit court where good-natured storytelling and plain old common sense won the case and the day. A high pile of papers made it clear that a lot of studying and preparation had gone into the case at hand. I guess this is what Mr. Lincoln meant when he said the studying paid off. Here he was, pleading a case before the highest court in the state, and looking quite at home doing it.[20]

December 31

New Year's Eve arrived and the town of Springfield celebrated in a royal manner. Although I resolved to study more in the year 1843, I decided not to get ahead of myself. So on December 31, I joined the other kids my age and did what we love to do best. Nothing like setting off fireworks to make you feel festive.

There was a splendid party going on at The American House. Mr. Sidney Breese had just been elected to the U.S. Congress, and was throwing this party to thank his supporters. Carriages, wagons and horses lined Adams Street, dropping off their gussied up ladies and gents. Seemed like the place was on fire, there were so many candles lighting the scene. Each time the door opened, music poured out as the cold air poured in. I could see that Judge Douglas, who lost the election, was there and taking an active part in the dancing. I reckon one good thing about losing is you don't have to pay for the celebration afterwards.

The night and the year ended with hurrahs at the stroke of twelve. It was time for me to get on home, and I was more than ready to tumble into bed and warm myself next to my little brother. But leg aches and tics were promising to keep me awake a while longer so I dug out this journal and set to write the final chapter of the year. Curiosity made me turn back to other months of 1842, and I soon found myself stifling gales of laughter in my pillow when I recalled the night the skunk got me when I tried to get him. I couldn't help but notice that my spelling and grammar had improved as the year went on, just like Mr. Lincoln said it would. Then I found myself quietly smiling as I read other things my friend Mr. Lincoln had said to me. The aching in my legs seemed to ease and my mind began to wander, dreaming of the day when Mr. Lincoln would be as proud of my friendship as I am of his.

Notes:

1. Letter to John T. Stuart, Jany. 23rd. 1841.
   "I am now the most miserable man living."
2. W. H .Herndon, *The Hidden Lincoln*, NY, Viking Press 1938, page 321
   Letter from R. B. Rutledge,
   "his practice was, when he wished to indelibly fix anything he was reading or studying on his mind,, to write it down, have known him to write whole pages of books he was reading."
3. Letter to Isham Reavis, Novr. 5-1855
4. Address to the Washington Temperance Society, February 22, 1842.
5. Letter to Joshua Speed, March 27th, 1842
6. Letter to Richard S. Thomas, Feb.14, 1843
   "Friend Richard... Now if you should hear any one say that Lincoln don't want to go to Congress, I wish you as a personal friend of mine, would you tell him you have reason to believe he is mistaken.. The truth is, I would like to go very much."
   Note: The first rail for the Northern Cross Railroad was put in place at Meredosia in 1837. By 1839, it was complete to Jacksonville and on February 15, 1842, the first train arrived in Springfield. In 1844, it was offered for sale, but decrepit and abandoned, there were no buyers.
7. May 5, 1842, Lincoln represented himself in Lincoln v Spencer Turner and Wm. Turner in DeWitt County. He was attempting to collect $200 due him.
8. Letter to Joseph Gillespie, July 13, 1849.
9. Pratt, Harry E. *,The Personal Finances of Abraham Lincoln,* The Abraham Lincoln Association, 1943.
10. *Collected Works of Abraham Lincoln,* ed. Roy P. Basler, 4:65.
11. Dennis Hanks to William Herndon, March 7 and 12, 1866.
12. Letter to Sangamo Journal, Sept. 2, 1842 , signed "Rebecca".

13. Donald, David Herbert, *Lincoln,*, Simon and Schuster, 1995, pp. 90-92. Abraham Lincoln and Mary Todd were renewing their friendship at this time after their long estrangement. It is believed that Mary Todd and her friend Julia Jayne were directly involved in these letters to the editor, but that Mr. Lincoln chose to accept the blame himself.
14. Turner and Turner, *Mary Todd Lincoln's Letters*, p.299. Years later when someone mentioned the duel to him, he said, "If you desire my friendship, you will never mention it again."
15. Peter's Pills advertised in about every issue of the Sangamo Journal in 1842
16. Baker, Jean H., *Mary Todd Lincoln*, page 97, W. W. Norton &Co., NY, 1987
17. McConnell, *Bunn Day Book*, 1840-43, p. 106
18. Keckley, Elizabeth, *Behind the Scenes*, G. W. Carlton, 1868, page 230.
    Also, Baker, page 85.
19. *Lincoln, Day by Day*, Harry E. Pratt, 1939, The Abraham Lincoln Association, Springfield. Monday, November 7, 1842, Logan and Lincoln have nine cases called on this one day term of Christian County Court.
20. *Lincoln Day by Day*. Friday, December 16, Averill v Field is argued before the court by Lincoln for the plaintiff.
21. *Here I Have Lived*, Paul M. Angle, 1935, The Abraham Lincoln Association. Page 99.

What Did Lincoln Do in 1862?

Betty Carlson Kay

January 1862

My Pa says there's more than one way to skin a cat
and so today when me and Willie tried to hitch up our goats to
our little cart and the axle broke, we just borrowed the laundry
woman's basket and hitched the goats up to it,
only she got really mad when we returned it caked in mud
and what have you
but what do you expect when the roads are as muddy
as the Potomac Flats?
We sure learned our lesson and when we go borrowing
something to replace our cart,
it won't be an old basket that wore out our bottoms
and only sat us one at a time.
But you never know what you're gonna see these days
just outside the White House yard
what with the Union soldiers camping in spitting distance
and me and Willie seen just about everything today when the
soldiers, naked as jay birds,
was having their weekly scrubbing
right in the freezy Potomac River.
Me and Willie, we are desperate to be Union soldiers
and whup the Confederate rebels
that plague our Pa but if we have to wash ourselves
in the icy, stinky river,
maybe we'll agree to wait a mite longer to fight for the Union.

Betty Carlson Kay

Pa takes his own good advice and tells his generals
that he don't care where they fight the secessionists,
or how they fight the secesh,
just as long as the Union stays together it's fine with him
but those generals he has right now are so plaguey slow
that Pa says "He would like to borrow" the Army of the Potomac
and lead it hisself for a while.[1]
Maybe if he was the General, instead of just the old President
of the United States,
he could get this Civil War over with and then
he wouldn't have so many meetings
and he'd have more time to play marbles with me and Willie.
When the rebs fired on Fort Sumter way back last April
and started this whole war,
most everybody thought that the fighting would be over
in a month or two easy,
but no one was counting on the South getting the smart generals
like Stonewall Jackson and Joe Johnston
and the Union army getting stuck
with pokey old General McClellan
who's been sick in bed for three weeks now
and always complaining about needing more horses and supplies
when don't he know, there ain't much money
for nothing anymore?
Such fussing over money betwixt Pa and his generals
and Ma and the shop keepers
and things must really be bad because Ma sent our nurse

What Did Lincoln Do in 1862?

back home to Springfield
when there wasn't enough money to pay her no longer.
Willie and me, we think that's just fine and now there's really
nobody watching us boys
and we can do whatever we want although Willie is so good that
sometimes he won't oblige me and do what I tell him to do
because now he's eleven
and thinks he's so smart because he can read and all
but even if I can't read yet and I talk funny,
Pa can understand me just fine and says,
"Let the boys be" when we get scolded.
Poor old Pa, he's so sad about the war these days,
he wants his boys to be happy no matter what we get up to.
Ma wants us to be happy too (and stay out of her way)
so one day she sewed me up a soldier uniform
just like the Zouaves from New York,
a shiny red and blue uniform that I want to wear every day,
and I *will* try to be good and stay out of the way
but don't you know there are people all over this house
and it's mighty hard not to get in somebody's way
what with folks standing in line to see Pa about
getting theirselves a job in his government
or about getting their kin a pardon
and the line gets so long it goes out his door,
across the hall and down the stairs,
and where are we supposed to play anyway?
Bud and Holly Taft come over just about every day

and our favorite game being soldiers, we give each other orders
(Willie's the Colonel, Bud is the Major, Holly is the Captain,
and I'm the drum major)
and march up and down the long halls
and climb up on the roof and make a fort up there
when the weather is nice.
If the weather is too cold we head up to our sitting rooms
and play with Willie's trains and if we are lucky
Pa comes in and we wrestle him to the floor
each one of us taking an arm or a leg til he cries Uncle.
Then we pretend to let him be
only we sneak right back up on him
and wrestle him all over again til his old sad face
don't look so sad no more.
Some days it gets so busy around here
that Pa says he feels like a hotel keeper
who's renting out rooms on one side of his hotel
while the other side burns down.
And one day everyone was busy doing something else
and no one was at the front door when it rang
so Willie went and opened it and who would have guessed
it would be a real Prince,
Prince Napoleon, nephew of Napoleon III,
that Willie would be bowing to,
as majestically as his eleven year old self could muster.
Even if he weren't very dressed up,
Willie did the best he could, and the Prince came right in,

"as if entering a café" he said in his diary.
So seems like Pa's right;
there's more than one way to skin a cat
like there's more than one way to open a door
and more than one way to fight a war.

February 1862

It was the last day of my childhood and I was too sick to know it.
Me and Willie, we did everything together
we even got sick together
like last year we both had measles
and Colonel Elmer Ellsworth caught 'em too,
being as he was around so much,
(why he even came out on the train with us
from back home in Illinois)
at least he *was* til the day he got hisself shot and killed
hauling down the Confederate flag over in Alexandria,
the same confederate flag I keep in my collection of stuff
and hang out once in a while
when I feel the need of a little attention.
Pa ached for him so that he allowed his funeral to be right here
in the White House.
And now this year me and Willie both had the fever.
Willie got sick first and I followed, like always,
only this time I wish I hadn't
and Willie he just got worse and worse

until he just couldn't fight no longer.

Ma and Pa didn't sleep for weeks

what with caring for us day and night

and then when Willie died Ma took to her room

and wouldn't come out

and Pa was left to bury Willie on a blustery day with only his oldest

son Bob to comfort him.

That old gale blew down a church on 13th street,

and the Potomac River rose up several feet,

high 'nuff for the water to splash over the Long Bridge

and the whole while poor Pa was trying to get Willie settled

into the burial vault that Mr. Carroll loaned us

so's we could take Willie back to Springfield with us

when we go home

and bury him proper there.

Ma and me waited in our rooms

feeling worse than I've ever felt in my whole born life.

Pa tried to care for me himself then,

even resting in bed with me at night

all the time wondering if I was gonna up and die too

which I didn't, I just got better and better

and soon I looked better than Pa

who hadn't slept in weeks

what with worrying about his boys at night

and worrying all day about his pokey generals

who never seemed to want to fight the rebels

or even chase them down.

When I was back on my feet Ma still couldn't stand to see anything
that reminded her of Willie
so Bud and Holly Taft were not allowed to come and play
and we gave away Willie's trains and tracks
so Ma wouldn't see her favorite boy's toys
and I had some long, lonely days with nobody to play with
and no where to go
seeing as Ma wasn't going no where like she used to,
like shopping in New York
or reading to soldier boys at the hospitals,
so I couldn't tag along with her like before
and I got the feeling that life as I knew it had changed for good.

March 1862

With me feeling a mite better, Pa would often times sleep
in his own room
with a sentry on duty in case some old assassin
wanted to slip in during the night and try to kill him,
so when I got to pining for Willie and needed to see my Pa
I slipped down the hall in my white nightshirt right past the sentry
and I used my special knock so Pa knew it were me
and not somebody out to kill him.
Three short knocks and two long knocks,
then I'd open the door and Pa would beckon me to come in
and it sure was a comfort to me
although I reckon Pa still lay there fretting about the soldier boys

Betty Carlson Kay

sleeping out on the ground in the cold and the wet
whilst we snuggled in warmth.
Why Pa fretted over everything these days
saving the Union being the most immediate thing
'cause if the Union failed,
why nothin' else could succeed, said he.
You could see in his eyes how much it mattered to him.
He carried a sadness around with him like his big gray shawl.
First things first, says Pa. Save the Union
and then the rest will all work out.
Like freeing them poor slaves who do all the heavy work
and get no pay at all for doing what nobody else wants to do.
Pa said that slavery was so wrong
that it would die of its own weight
which I don't quite believe
because Judge David Davis from back home in Illinois
why he is the biggest, fattest man I know
and even he don't die of his own weight.
So why did Pa think slavery would die when the slaves don't
weigh near as much as the Judge?
Old Abe don't think there's much good about slavery at all.
Said that unless someone wants to be a slave themselves,
they shouldn't oughta have slaves of their own.
Me? Heck no, I don't want to be no man's slave.
I'd mind the work plenty but most of all
I'd mind being sold away from my Ma and Pa.
That don't sound a mite Christian to me.

Sometimes when I go to Sunday School with Bud and Holly Taft,
I vex the teacher pretty bad with all my questions about a god
who could allow a wee child to be sold away from his Ma and Pa
and sometimes the teacher asks me to just keep my questions
to myself and quit interrupting her lesson
but it seems to me that the only way to find something out
is to ask questions.
Right now my Pa is fit to be tied over his General McClellan
who has "the slows" and don't seem to want to fight.
Seems Mac thought the rebs had them outgunned
over there towards Manasses
so after fixin' to attack, he changed his mind
only to find out later that lots of the guns were just logs
pointed to look like guns
and the thousands of rebel soldiers the Union kept counting
were the same rebs in different places
getting counted again and again.
What a tricky bunch them rebels are!
They sure tricked ol' Mac.
Pa just sat with his head in his huge hands and most nearly cried.
And the plaguey war goes on.

April 1862

My birthday came and went with hardly nobody noticing.
April 4th was just like any other day
'cept I was now nine and I determined to act more like Willie

and less like the old Taddie.

Seems hard to believe that the war's been going on

a full year now and

the north ain't got much to show for it.

Just last April when the rebels fired on Fort Sumter

and started this whole mess

Pa had volunteers sign up for three months,

'Cause they was all so sure that the war would be over

in nothin' flat.

Seems like a lot of folks were fooled on that score.

Now the rebs got theirselves an old, used Federal ship

used to be called the *Merrimack* and

now they call it the *Virginia*.

They covered it with iron

so as gun shot just bounces off of it

and they are creating quite a panic on the Union's ships

when the shells start flying

and the plain wooden boats catch fire

and the *Virginia* she just goes on her way

like she owns the whole Potomac River

and watches while the Union boats burn and sink.

Pa says those confederates are doing a few things right

and I reckon covering a ship with iron

like the knights in shining armor used to cover theirselves

is a pretty fine idea.

Maybe the Union oughta get theirselves

a whole bunch of ironclads too.

What Did Lincoln Do in 1862?

Then we'd whup them rebs good.
Pa don't even like to call the rebs by their fancy name,
The Confederate States of America,
says it ain't the truth when the rebs call theirselves that
'Cause there ain't no such thing
as seceding from the Union
and making theirselves a separate country.
Just 'cause you call something a fancy name
don't make it true, he says.
Pa says it's like asking,
"How many legs would my goat have
if I called his tail a leg?"
He'd still have 4 legs!
Just 'cause you call a tail a leg don't make it so.
Just 'cause they call theirselves a country
don't make it one neither.
So Old Abe, he always calls them
"the so-called Confederate states".
Then they never get to thinking that he believes
they have their own country.
The weather got to warming itself up the other day
and I tried to have me some fun.
I found my soldier doll and played like the rebs shot him
and there weren't no Union men there to bury him fine
so the rebs, they quick buried him in a shallow grave face down.
I only messed up a few roses trying to get him buried but
when the gardener caught me, he scolded me from here to there

not just about the roses but about

the *indignity* toward the dead of burying them face down

and when I said What does it matter if'n a body is already dead

which way they bury it?

He told me he'd never before met a boy with such bad manners.

Maybe my manners would be better if Willie was still here.

He always was a better boy than I was.

May 1862

Sure wish Pa would take me with him

when he goes off to have some fun

like the other night when he and Mr. Chase and Mr. Stanton

decided to see the fighting scene of operations for theirselves

and they all got on the Treasury's cutter, *Miami,*

and sailed off down the Potomac all the way to Fort Monroe.

Everybody told my Pa that he couldn't land troops

anywheres near the town of Norfolk

but my Pa he thinks for hisself and he looked at lots of maps

and got a little tugboat to take him and Mr. Stanton

right up on the Virginia shore

in the middle of the night

and don't you know my Pa insisted on getting off the tug

and walking right on that sacred sesech land

in the light of the moon,

right under the very noses of them rebs and they never know'd it!

Hah! Next day, the soldiers took Pa's good advice

What Did Lincoln Do in 1862?

and they had hardly landed
afore those confederates surrendered.
Then, kaboom, the pesky, ironclad *Virginia* was blown up
and would never shoot at the Union blockade again.
I begged and begged Pa to take me with him
when he goes and has his adventures,
but no such luck, he leaves me at home with nothing to do
and nobody to do nothin' with
so how *am* I supposed to stay out of trouble?
I just wish Pa wasn't so sad all the time.
The best part is late at night when he can't sleep
and I feel him crawl into bed with me.
That's when I can whisper him my secrets
and he can whisper me his
although it gets a mite close in my little bed, as anyone can tell,
being that he is so big and all.
He says it comforts him some to lie next to his boy but I know
he's still thinking about Willie and pining for him like I do
only he tries so hard not to show it especially to Ma
who won't somedays get out of bed
and most never comes out of her room.
I say it's good that now she never catches me
and scolds me for my bad manners,
but Pa and I both know it ain't good and we sure hope
she gets to feeling stronger soon.
Last night he shook my little bed laughing so hard
over another adventure he had when he was out

Betty Carlson Kay

checking on his soldiers again.
Seems like they were building a trestle bridge a hundred feet
above the water over a ravine
and my Pa wanted to talk to the soldiers on the far side
so he said to Mr. Stanton and Officer Dahlgren
that he fancied he'd just walk
over to the other side on the one plank they had finished
and, course, those other two men couldn't let him go on alone
and so they both followed him dizzy as could be
and needing to help each other on the way
but my Pa he just walked the plank all the way
like he was crossing a creek back home in Illinois
and there was nothing to it.
I sure wish I could've seen their faces.
Pa took great pleasure in relating that tale
but now I've got myself an idea about walking a plank
set up on the roof of this mansion,
up where I have my cannons and guns and all
and I'll probably get in trouble for doing the exact same thing
my Pa thinks is so hilarious.
Seems like grown ups get all the fun.[2]

June 1862

My Ma's black barouche came around most every day lately
and picked her up at the front door of the White House
and at first Ma was most secretive about where she was going.

So I was fixin' to sneak onto the backside of the coach
and hold on tight
and tag along without her knowin'
when lo and behold one day Yib Keckley slipped
and said something 'bout Ma goin' to talk to Willie!
Well, if Ma was talking to Willie seemed only fair
I should up and join her and talk to him too
but Ma caught me sneakin' around and confessed
that she'd been talkin' to Willie through some mediums
over in Georgetown named Mr. and Mrs. Cranston Laurie
who could put her in touch with both her favorite Willie
and her dear little Eddie
who'd been gone all these many years.
Seems these mediums believe that when a body dies
they shed their human body like a snake sheds his skin
but then their spirits keep coming around waiting
for living folks to contact them.
Ma always did believe a little in spiritualists
even back home in Springfield
maybe even more than she believed in the Presbyterianists
and so day after day she'd been going to the Laurie house
and sitting round the dining room table
with only a candle to give a bit of light
and somedays Ma was able to talk direct to Willie
which would raise her spirits even higher
than it would raise Willie's
and she would come back home almost happy.

Betty Carlson Kay

But sometimes when Willie was unavailable,

instead some other dead soldiers would talk with her

and give her advice about the war to tell Pa.

Ma says that sometimes lately she don't even need no medium

to help her reach Willie

she could do it all by herself.

She could make Willie come and stand

at the end of the bed in her room

and sometimes he'd bring Eddie and they'd both smile at her

and for a few minutes Ma would have

her one big happy family together again.

Then she'd be all excited and tell Pa the wonderful news

that Willie and Eddie were smiling and happy

and Pa would hold onto her hand and smile that sad smile

that seemed more like crying than smiling and said

There, there Mother, it'll be all right.

Then she'd go on off to bed and Pa would sit there all night

never moving til morning, I do believe,

'cause he'd still be there looking tired and sad and old

when I got up the next day.

Pa suggested a change of scenery

like out to the countryside just north of the White House

where we could all breathe some fresh air

and be far away from the memories

that haunted the rooms of the Executive Mansion.

Seems to me no matter where I go

I'll be just as lonely 'cause Willie ain't really comin' back
no matter what Ma says she sees.

July 1862

Summer seemed hotter than ever
in the White House in Washington City
so Ma and Pa and me and 19 wagon loads of stuff
headed out of town
to stay a while at the Soldiers' Home just north of town.
Three miles seemed far away from the war, at least to me,
but Pa he got up early
and rode his horse to town most every day,
and times was that the Secretary of State, Mr. Seward,
rode his horse out to meet with Pa at the Soldiers' Home
in the daylight or by the starlight
and they never was afraid of no assassins on the road
along the way.
See, the first time we came to Washington City
on the train with Mr. Elsworth and all,
why some men told Pa that some assassins would get him
as he rode through Baltimore City
so Pa he disguised himself and bent way low
so as to hide his great height
and then he rode on a different train from our family
and kind of slipped into Washington safe and sound.
But you know, some folks who don't much like my Pa

they said he was cowardly for that
and now he tries never to act afraid even when he is.
So it was pretty nice up on that wooded hill
and we could breathe the clean fresh air again
that don't smell like no latrines
and most nearly pretend the war wasn't of much count
and Ma seemed to raise herself up a bit out of her gloom.
Yib Keckley went with us to sew Ma's clothes
and keep her company.
Those two are like peas in a pod
they spend so much time together
and 'course they do a fair amount of talking.
Seems like they understand each other
since they's both lost a dear boy lately
as Yib's son was killed in the fightin' back in Missouri a while ago
and it don't seem to make no never mind that Yib is a Negro
and a dressmaker and Ma's the First Lady of the United States
why Yib is the best friend Ma has,
even better than her own sisters
who sometimes don't appreciate Ma.
I can't say her real name, Lizzie nor Elizabeth, like Ma and Pa
but she don't seem to mind one bit if I just call her Yib.
She still talks to me like I was just as good as Willie
even when I get excited and silly
and she never tries to make me practice her name right.

August 1862

People were always giving me and Willie presents
like our goats and the pony
and even now that it's just me, they still like to give presents.
That ain't bad 'cept I wish Willie were here
to share the presents with.
Somebody gave me a big red, silk balloon one day
and it 'minded me of the huge balloons belonging to one
Colonel Thaddeus Lowe who brought his hot air balloons
right here to the White House lawn to show my Pa
how they could be of help to the Union army
during this here current *unpleasantness.*
(That's the word some southern folks like to use
to describe the Civil War they started.
Guess they don't like to 'fess up to starting no war.)
Anyways, this Colonel Lowe is kind of a magician with all his ideas
and inventions and with his flair for the unusual.
One time, afore this war really started in earnest,
he accidently flew his balloon
from Cincinnati all the way to South Carolina
still dressed for dinner in a top hat and fancy suit
and those rebels they 'most nearly killed him for being a Yankee.
Sounds like something dumb me and Willie would do
if he was still here.
Anyway, when the war got itself really going,

Betty Carlson Kay

Mr. Lowe got hisself the idea that he could use his balloons

to help the Union Army see just exactly

what those rebs were doing

by flying up high and scouting the area from a bird's eye view.

So Mr. Lowe he comes to Washington

and shows off his balloons by

flying them on the lawn of the new Smithsonian Museum

and the Capitol

and even the White House.

That was the day we could see them the best

with the big silky balloons and the long ropes

and the baskets holding him up.

My Pa kind of likes inventions and new ideas

and he says to Mr. Lowe

You can be a Colonel of the Balloon Corps.

So Colonel Lowe takes all his balloons

and heads right near the battle fields in Virginia

and from up high he sends messages to the army and tells them

which way the rebs are heading.

One of his balloons has a BIG picture of General McClellan

painted on its side

only even with a big picture of himself flying in the sky

McClellan still is slow as molasses in January.

The rebs really don't like Colonel Lowe

minding *their* business from above

and they's always trying to shoot him down.

Why he says he's the most shot at man in the whole army!

And sometimes the shots hit the basket or the ropes
but then he does some mighty tricky maneuvering
and so far they ain't hit him.
'Course those secesh start to wondering
how they can get a balloon too
'cept they ain't got enough money to buy the fancy silk by the yard
so they made their own silk balloon out of ladies' silk dresses
and their balloon was the most colorful thing
anyone ever laid their eyes on
only it didn't last long 'cause the Federals captured it one day
whilst they was floating it down the river closer to a battle.
And Colonel Lowe, he cut it all up
and gave away the pieces of silk as souvenirs
only I reckon the soldiers used the silk for handkerchiefs and
bandages and what have you.
So when I got my red balloon
I decided I'd do a little reconnaissance for myself
so I climbed up to the roof of the Soldiers' Home
and set off to check where the rebs were.
Only that red balloon really disappointed me
and not only didn't it fly UP
it barely slowed my progress DOWN.
The gardener who doesn't much like me
didn't look all that concerned
so I brushed myself off and went to find Jack.
Maybe he could do a little scouting better than I could.[3]
I asked Pa a really hard question today

one of those questions that makes my
Sunday School teacher frown,
about how the North thinks that God is on *their* side in this war
and how the South thinks that God is on *their* side
and how can God be on *both* sides
and Pa gives me that really sad look again
and says that God cannot be *for* and *against* the same thing
at the same time.
Who knows? He says. Maybe God's purpose is different
from the purpose of either side.
So I guess we just need to keep trying to figure out
what God's got in mind.[4]
But I think I'll leave that up to Pa as it seems a bit much for me.

September 1862

Even if he can't find hisself a fightin' general,
at least Old Abe has finally found a *Colonel* who fights
to his satisfaction.
Colonel Benjamin Grierson is his name and don'tcha know?
He's from back home in Illinois!
Yup, and he leads his 6th Illinois Cavalry
right straight into rebel territory
'way down in Miss'ippi
and keeps nipping at them rebels' heels
like a dog who won't let go of his bone.
Yessiree, he don't jest let them rebs retreat,

(like some other generals we know)
he chases them down and burns their railway depots,
captures their horses and takes prisoners.
His cavalry is clearing a path for some major Illinois troops
led by a General Grant and a Brigadier General Sherman,
so they can split the south and win the war.
This here Colonel Grierson leads the cavalry charge on
"Old Barber" and wears a white duster
which kind of makes him easy to see
and his coat and his horse are suffering holes from secesh guns.
But he don't quit.
Just like my Pa would do if'n he were a soldier.
My Pa and Colonel Grierson would have grand times together
fightin' all day and playin' with their boys in betwixt times-
Yep, Pa says that Mrs. Grierson comes right to the campgrounds
and lets the boys play with their Pa
whilst she mixes up some mince meat pies for supper.
Ma says to hush and don't ever dream of such a thing
but Pa and me that's what we call fun.
Why Colonel Grierson could even sing
those funny ol' songs Pa loves,
being as he is a band leader and song writer from Jacksonville.[5]
Then maybe Old Abe would wear a smile
that reaches down to his heart,
'stead of plastering on a half smile that don't fool nobody.
"Old Abe Lincoln came out of the wilderness"
that's what they'd sing like they did back home

when he was first nominated to be President
when 6,000 marchers took 2 ½ hours to pass
by our house on 8th Street
wearing "Wide Awake" capes and caps
and holding up kerosene torches and singing mightily,
'specially when they seen Old Abe standing out on the porch.
Sometimes I wish we could be back at home with just our family
and Willie would still be here
and Bob would come home and visit from Harvard
and we'd still be happy and carefree.
That's the word: carefree.
Seems like a long time since we been free of cares.
Betwixt Willie dying and the war killing so many boys
and Pa fretting about the generals
and Ma being heartbroken
makes me wish we never'd set our eyes on this town.

October 1862

Seems as if Pa is fixin' to make a fancy new law
come January first
which he thinks will help the slaves get theirselves free
in the South and end the war.
It's got a pretty fancy name, *The Emancipation Proclamation*,
and Pa's been workin' on it a long time.
That and walking back and forth to the War Department
has occupied him for quite some time now.

He likes to be in the telegraph office hisself
to get the telegrams when they first arrive
click- clacking over the wires
with news of the battles and casualties.
Then he likes to send congratulations
or more likely *suggestions* to the pokey generals
if he thinks they ain't doin' much good.
Sometimes I wait with Pa in the telegraph office
and if I fall asleep in front of the fireplace before he's ready to go
he carries me home and puts me to bed
before he lets his old bones rest.
Then he's up and gone long before I am,
having his egg for breakfast and a cup of coffee
and though he's looking thinner and thinner
he won't hardly take the time to eat ever.
Most nights he don't come home til 11 o'clock
and Ma she tries to be there to make him feel like
Home Sweet Home
and give him some comfort when she's hardly got any to spare.
Seems like sometimes there ain't no hope
for this war never ending.
Pa can't figure out why McClellan won't fight.
Why ever since Antietam five weeks ago
there's been no action on the part of Old Mac
except to complain that his horses are sore tongued
and fatigued.
So my Pa asked the General

"what the horses have done since the battle of Antietam
that fatigue anything?"[6]
Then the General acts all insulted and Pa ends up apologizing
for hurting his feelings
when I would've told him different.
But my Pa, he's trying to keep his generals happy,
and keep the North happy
and the border states happy
so as to keep the *old* soldiers happy
and the *new* soldiers volunteering
and maybe get to the end of this here war.
Then there comes a day when
a bit of good news comes across the wires
and a smile almost makes it across Pa's face
and he says that maybe hope is not completely lost.

November 1862

Finally my Pa couldn't stand it no longer and
General McClellan ain't no longer in charge of the Union Forces.
Pa told General Burnside to be in charge
and who knows? Maybe he'll do the trick.
This time when Ma made a trip north to New York
she let me come along thinking it might take my mind off
my awful lonesomeness.
I wish she'd let Bud and Holly Taft come play again,
but now we hear tell

What Did Lincoln Do in 1862?

that they are being sent north to school

so I won't never play with them again.

I had to try to stand real still while I got measured

for two new suits of clothes

and I can't say it did much to cheer me up

to be told over and over

to *please* stand still

but I got the plaguey new suits

and somedays it seems like Ma's happy

and then she has her bad days and it's a good thing

Yib Keckley went with us

'cause I don't seem to help Ma's nerves at all.

Not like Willie used to. And Yib does now.

I lost a tooth and Ma sent it in a letter to Pa

so's he'd know we still miss him and all.

Ma and Mrs. Keckley spend most of their time together.

Mrs. Keckley is no different than a white woman

on the inside says Ma

and a whole lot better than many fancy ladies

who only look good on the outside

but ain't so nice on their insides.

And Ma, she's talking more and more like an abolitionist,

which is a mite surprising from a Kentucky gal

who grew up with slaves in her house.

There's a lot of slaves freeing theirselves these days

and running north with the help of Union soldiers

making camps conveniently close to their old plantations.

When the slaves slip into the camps of the Army of the Potomac
ain't many soldiers mean enough
to make them go back to slavery
so the slaves just hang around in the camps
or get theirselves to Washington City where they gather together
but with winter coming on, their lack of both money and jobs
ain't doin' them no favors
and Mrs. Keckley and Ma why they're up to something all the time
like trying to get blankets for the "contrabands"
to get them through the winter.
And Ma is always writing a letter asking a favor for somebody;
sometimes it's even a job for an ex-slave
and sometimes she gets them a job and don't Ma look pleased.
Ma says Pa's doing the right thing fixing to free the slaves
in the rebel territories
but lots of them have already emancipated theirselves
right into the army camps
and into the city of Washington way ahead of Pa.

December 1862

Seems like the whole country is full of trouble
and not just with the old seceshes down South.
Now Pa is fretting over the Sioux Indians
way out west in Minnesota.
Can't nobody get along at all?
Seems like there's no way one person can take care

What Did Lincoln Do in 1862?

of all the problems in this here country
even if that one person *is* the President of the United States.
Now the injuns have been fightin' with the settlers
over broken treaty rights and land promises
and for a while it looked like the injuns were winning
but then Pa sent General Pope,
after he lost the second Battle of Bull Run,
out to settle it all down but then it turns out
General Pope wants to hang all the injuns
who was doing the fightin'
and Pa he says we don't hang all the secesh rebs
so how can we hang all the indian rebels?
So there sits Pa day after day reading papers full of injun names
that *nobody* can't hardly read not just me!
And he's fixin' to hang a lot less than the 300
that General Pope wants him to.
The Governor of Minnesota even said Pa'd get more votes
in the next election
if he hanged more injuns
but my Pa he ain't so fond of killing these days.
Besides, he heard tell that the starving injuns
were just trying to get food for their families
and Pa says he reckons that not many of them
were really murderers.
Thirty eight men hanging is a sight less than 300
but I still think it would be a sight worth seeing.
Guess Minnesota is a might too far to visit just to see a hanging

and even I am getting tired of all this killing business.
I'm fixin' to put away my uniform for a while and
let Jack go on furlough too.
Seems to me the whole country could use a furlough
from this here Civil War.
Time to say good-bye to 1862
and welcome to 1863.
Tomorrow Pa will have a big reception
and shake hands with anybody who wants to come see him
at the White House and wish him a happy new year
and his hand will probably be all sore and puffy
from all that handshaking
but Pa says he's gonna sign the Emancipation Proclamation
first thing in the morning before his hands swell up
and make his writing look shabby.
Maybe he'll sign the fancy paper
and after that even more Negroes will fight for the Union
and the war will be over in no time.
Then maybe 1863 won't be so full of sadness and dying
as this year.
Can't say I'm sorry to say good-bye to 1862.

The Story Ends

On January 1, 1863, President Lincoln signed the Emancipation Proclamation, freeing the slaves in the rebel states. He didn't sign it first thing in the morning, due to a printing error, and by the time he signed it, his hand *was* swollen and his penmanship *was* shabby. Opinion varied. Some said he should have freed the slaves sooner; some said he should have waited longer. But the *political* Lincoln signed the proclamation at just the right time. The border states did not cross over to the Confederacy; many freed slaves joined the Union forces; and the war was finally won in April 1865. The 13th Amendment to the Constitution eventually freed all the slaves in the re-united United States.

The President and his wife and their two sons, Tad and Robert, enjoyed the celebrations marking the end of the long conflict, knowing that the goal of saving the Union had been achieved. The few days of celebration abruptly ended when John Wilkes Booth shot the President while he and Mary Lincoln were enjoying the play, *Our American Cousin*, at Ford's Theater on April 14, 1865. President Lincoln died the following day.

The train that carried Lincoln's body back to Springfield also carried Willie's smaller coffin, and thus the two of them returned to their home together. They were buried in Oak Ridge cemetery.

Tad and his mother traveled in the United States and Europe during the lonely years that followed, while Robert married and started his own family. Soon Tad fell ill with pleurisy and died at the age of eighteen, in 1871. He joined his father and brothers in the Lincoln family tomb in Springfield.

Mrs. Lincoln spent her last years very much alone and lonely. She died in 1882 in the same Springfield home she had been married in forty years before.

Robert lived until 1926, and since *his own* son had already died, there was no male heir to carry on the Lincoln name, in the traditional way of sons carrying on the family name.

Notes:

1. Irwin McDowell's Diary account in William Swinton, <u>Campaigns of the Army of the Potomac</u>, NY Charles B Richardson, 1866, Pp. 79-82.
2. Herbert, David Donald, <u>Lincoln</u>, page 352.
3. Block, Eugene B., <u>Above the Civil War, The Story of Thaddeus Lowe</u>, Howell-North Books, Berkeley, CA, 1966.
4. Lincoln, Abraham, *Meditations on the Divine Will*, early September 1862, Speeches and Writings 1859-1865, Library of America, 1989.
5. Leckie, William H. and Shirley A., <u>Unlikely Warriors</u>, <u>General Benjamin Grierson and His Family,</u> University of Oklahoma Press, Norman, OK, 1984, pp.70-74.
6. Letter to Majr. Genl. McClellan from A. Lincoln on October 25, 1862, <u>Lincoln, Speeches and Letters</u>, Library of America, 1989.

About the Author

Teaching elementary school for 34 years has given **Betty Carlson Kay** a sense of what is needed to enhance and expand existing curriculum. So far, she is the author of 8 books for children, including *Illinois from A to Z.* Previous books about Abraham Lincoln include a counting book and an alphabet book. In this volume, she has researched Lincoln's life in New Salem, Illinois, Springfield, Illinois and Washington, D.C. The stories of three pivotal years in his life are told month-by-month through the eyes of children who knew him.

Betty Kay was born and raised in Cicero, Illinois, where she attended Morton East High School. After college at Iowa State University and University of Iowa, she taught first grade in the Springfield Public Schools and added a Master's Degree at the University of Illinois. She is now happily retired in Jacksonville, Illinois with her husband, John. Being a grandmother is the best thing that has ever happened to her!

Printed in the United States
49818LVS00002B/307-510